the MINIVERS ON THE RUN

Australian praise for *The Minivers*:

ABANDONED!

Mystery surrounds the origins of a miniature baby girl discovered in a shoe box outside the Artemisia Hospital on Thursday night. The newborn, who weighs about the same as a block of butter, is in excellent health according to doctors, who can find no explanation for her unusual size.

The baby has stolen the hearts of Artemisians, with dozens of families already offering to adopt her. Meanwhile, the hospital has renewed appeals for the baby's parents to come forward.

MINIATURE BABY HEADED FOR PALACE!

It's official. In a move that will disappoint hundreds of hopeful families, Papa King announced last night that he will be fostering Artemisia's famous miniature orphan himself.

'It's my job to look after all disadvantaged citizens,' the king said. 'I am determined that this tiny abandoned baby will have the chance she deserves.' Artemisia's ruler has already chosen his new baby's name. From now on, she will be called Rosamund, after his mother, the late queen; and Miniver because she is a 'miniature version' of a human being.

A sister for Rosamund

Now there are two of us! Artemisia's darling, Rosamund Miniver, is pictured here with her new miniature sister, Emily, who was found in a basket on the steps of Miniver House yesterday morning.

'The baby is absolutely gorgeous,' said excited foster father Papa King. 'Rosamund is so excited, she won't leave Emily alone. Now there's another Miniver for Artemisians to love.'

Emily

Sweet and fresh as a
Miniver Morning
A new perfume from
Delaney's of Queen Street

It's a Miniver Morning

'Miniver Morning', Rosamund Miniver's first single, has debuted at Number 1 in the Artemisia charts.

'I'd like to dedicate the song to my little sister Emily,' Rosamund told Pop Music Weekly. The miniature pop star ruled out the possibility of a concert tour, as four-year-old Emily is too young to go with her. 'We Minivers do everything together,' Rosamund said. 'I can't travel anywhere without Emily. It would be awful.'

MINIVER HOUSE DECOR SETS NEW TRENDS

PINK IS THE NEW COLOUR for home this summer, with the Miniver sisters' announcement that the outside of Miniver House is being completely repainted in blush pink. The pink accents continue inside the miniature mansion, where new rose-coloured living-room carpet will be highlighted by green and white. Rumour has it that Rosamund, who favours bold colours, has ordered cerise and gold furnishings for her gorgeous turret bedroom. Since Minivers love to do everything together, our guess is Emily's room is being redecorated to match in her favourite turquoise blue.

MINIVERS CONCERT BREAKS ALL RECORDS

More than twenty thousand people braved thunderstorms to attend a rare Minivers live concert at the Artemisia Cricket Ground last night. Watched by Papa King and backed by a thirteen piece band, the miniature singing sensations wowed their audience with hits, including their latest Number 1, 'Sisters Forever' from the album Minivers Together. The televised event was watched by an estimated 85% of the viewing audience, the most ever recorded.

HIT MINIVER
TV SERIES RETURNS

CHANNEL 6 has confirmed that the Miniver sisters will return to Artemisia's screen for another ten episodes of *The Minivers' Music Hour* in the New Year. The third series of the successful programme will show the Minivers performing in the studio, and give never-before-seen glimpses of the famously close sisters' private life. Filming has already begun and the first episode will be shown in early February.

PAPA KING HAS STROKE

Papa King remains in a serious condition following a stroke late yesterday afternoon. A palace official has confirmed that Artemisia's ruler was unconscious when he was taken to the Royal Artemisia Hospital shortly before six o'clock.

Papa King had been entertaining his foster daughters, the famous Miniver sisters, but is believed to have been alone when the stroke occurred. A spokeswoman said that the Minivers were trying to comfort each other. 'They are shocked, because they are fond of Papa King. They hope he will be better soon.'

Doctors say it is too early to know whether Papa King will recover.

Natalie Jane Prior was born in Brisbane, Australia, in November, 1963. Her father is English, and her mother Australian. As a child, she spent most of her time with her nose in a book, or writing doll-sized stories for her friends during maths lessons. She made up her mind to be a children's author when she was about ten, and although she worked for a while as a librarian for a gold-mining company, she has never seriously wanted to do anything else.

Natalie published her first book, *The Amazing Adventures of Amabel,* in 1990. Since then she has written picture books, prize-winning novels and even a best-selling book about mummies! Some of her other books include *The Paw* (illustrated by Terry Denton), a picture book about a cat burglar, and the *Lily Quench* series, which has been published in many countries around the world. Natalie started working on the *Minivers* because she wanted to write a book about what it's like to be on the run when you're only two feet tall and everyone knows what you look like.

Natalie lives in Brisbane with her husband and daughter and two miniature dachshunds called Rupert and Jasmine, in a house with a dragon on the roof.

the MINIVERS
ON THE RUN

Natalie Jane Prior

mlb
MARION LLOYD BOOKS

First published in the UK in 2010 by Marion Lloyd Books
An imprint of Scholastic Children's Books
Euston House, 24 Eversholt Street
London, NW1 1DB, UK
A division of Scholastic Ltd.
Registered office: Westfield Road, Southam, Warwickshire, CV47 0RA
SCHOLASTIC and associated logos are trademarks and/or
registered trademarks of Scholastic Inc.

ISBN 9781407110448

A CIP catalogue record for this book is available
from the British Library

Printed and bound in Great Britain by
CPI Bookmarque, Croydon CR0 4TD
Papers used by Scholastic Children's Books are made from
wood grown in sustainable forests.

1 3 5 7 9 10 8 6 4 2

www.scholastic.co.uk/zone

For Margaret Connolly

1

THE BIRTHDAY

It was eight o'clock, and the fans outside the hotel on Miniver Boulevard had been milling about behind the barriers for hours. It was a hot night and there were the first rumblings of a thunderstorm. The people at the front, who were squashed up against the crowd fences and actually had a chance of seeing the Minivers when they arrived, had been sprayed several times with water to keep them from fainting. The news helicopters, buzzing overhead, sent warm air gusting over the greasy pavements and swept their searchlights over the glass and chrome frontages of the surrounding buildings.

Walkie-talkies clicked and crackled. Security men in blue uniforms looked anxiously at the crowd barriers and stopped the fans who were silly enough to try and jump them. From time to time, limousines pulled up at the end of the long red carpet. Each time this happened, there was a flurry of excitement, but the people who got out were only guests, who passed quickly through the waiting news crews and went into the hotel. In the foyer, encased in perspex and surrounded by admirers, was a shoe box. It was nothing special, just a little red and blue battered bit of cardboard, but it had a security guard all to itself, and from the look on his face and the gun in his belt, it was clear that he meant business.

Soon after eight o'clock, a roar went up at the far end of Miniver Boulevard. This time there was no mistake, for the car had a red flag with the sweeping initial *M* on the bonnet.

"It's them! It's them! It's the Minivers!" cried the crowd. As the great black limousine crawled, bit by bit, towards the hotel, the fans swelled forward until the barriers rocked and sent the security guards scurrying to hold them back. By the time the limousine pulled up at the red carpet, the screams were so deafening it was hard to believe they could get louder. But they did, as the driver got out of the car and produced a step; they got louder again as he put the step beside the rear passenger door, and when he opened the door and Rosamund Miniver climbed out of the car, they echoed off the surrounding buildings until it sounded as if their glass fronts must shatter and the whole lot fall down in a heap.

Rosamund Miniver was wearing a red silk halter-neck dress, covered with sequins that caught the flash of a thousand cameras. The rich colour made her pale skin look paler, and her dark hair and eyes even darker than they were. A smile broke over her lovely face at the sound of the cheers, and she lifted a small white hand in acknowledgement.

Her sister Emily followed, dressed in shimmering green, with gold sandals on her feet and dozens of sparkling butterflies scattered through her hair. The fans roared, and the Minivers paused to wave again and blow kisses.

"Rosamund! Rosamund! Happy birthday, Rosamund! We love you, Rosamund! Emily! Emily, we love you, too!"

The two girls linked hands and walked towards the building. Unable to see them, the fans at the back started jostling for position. Children and grown-ups alike were pushed forward, fainting and screaming, until the fences bulged and threatened to give way.

"Rosamund! Emily!" they sobbed, as the Minivers disappeared into the building. "Come back!" A few people climbed on each other's shoulders to catch one final glimpse, but for most of them, it was hopeless. For Rosamund and Emily Miniver, though slim, dark-haired and beautiful, were not like any other girls alive.

The most famous people in Artemisia were only two feet tall.

"Stupid old thing," muttered Rosamund Miniver, as she and her sister were escorted by Ron, their Chief of Security, past the perspex case in the foyer. "I don't know why everyone gets so excited about it. It's just a shoe box, after all."

"It's *your* shoe box, Rose," said Emily. "Don't forget, most people only get to see it once a year. Of course they find it exciting."

Rosamund and Emily walked towards the ballroom. As its golden doors were flung open, there was a cascade of applause and a blinding battery of camera flashes. A floodlight swung down from the ceiling to highlight their diminutive figures and the band, which had been playing jazzed-up versions of famous Minivers songs, started playing "Happy Birthday" instead.

It was Rosamund Miniver's fourteenth birthday. Fourteen years ago she had been found on the steps of the Artemisia Hospital in the same battered shoe box that the fans were admiring in the foyer. The nurse who found the box had been in the very act of dropping it in the rubbish when a faint cry from inside caught her attention. When she removed the lid, she had discovered a tiny naked baby, so small she could have fitted into a child's plimsoll. That was why Rosamund, and later Emily, had been given the surname Miniver. It had been chosen for them by their foster father,

Artemisia's ruler, Papa King, because they were miniature versions of human beings.

Emily's arrival had been less spectacular. She had turned up four years later in a rush basket on the steps of Miniver House, the miniature mansion Papa King had built for Rosamund to live in with her housekeeper, Millamant. Emily and Rosamund had been together, ever since. When Emily was unhappy, it was Rosamund who made her laugh again; and it was Emily who stopped Rosamund from getting worked up and upset.

Hand in hand, the Miniver sisters made their way through the adoring guests to a central dais. Here, raised above the floor so that they would be on the same level as everyone else, were their miniature dining table and chairs, and, on a separate table, Rosamund's birthday cake. Millamant had made it in three pink tiers, with real sugared roses falling in waterfalls down its sides. The dais overflowed with presents, and in the midst of everything stood a very small woman, Millamant herself. She was wearing a blue dress and flat satin shoes, and her blonde plaits were pinned across the top of her head. She looked, as she usually did, like a tiny human bulldog.

"Milly! What a beautiful job!" Rosamund climbed the steps and kissed her. "Real roses, too! Look, Emmie, isn't she clever?"

Millamant went pink. Emily guessed that she, too, had

been pleased with the roses, though being Millamant, she would rather have died than admit the fact. Suddenly another voice spoke directly behind them. Emily jumped.

"Good evening, Rosamund, Emily."

A pale woman with drab brown hair had walked, completely uninvited, up the steps. It was Papa King's daughter Karen, known as Madame. She was standing extremely close and Emily edged protectively nearer to Rosamund's elbow. Something about Madame always made the Minivers feel nervous, though there was no real reason why it should.

"I didn't realize you were coming, Madame," said Rosamund. "Did we send you an invitation?"

Madame's plain face flushed unattractively. "Oh, yes," she said. "Papa King sends you his good wishes – and this present." She produced a small pink parcel from her handbag and handed it over with some reluctance.

Rosamund's guard immediately dropped. "From Papa King?"

Ever since Papa King had become ill and Madame had returned from her mysterious exile, Rosamund and Emily had scarcely seen their foster father. Rosamund, who had always adored him, had gone to the palace once and insisted on visiting him. She had come home very upset. Papa King, she had told Emily, was attached to a machine that did his breathing for him, and he had not even recognized her. But if Papa King had remembered her birthday, perhaps he was getting better. Rosamund ripped the gift wrap off the parcel and eagerly opened the tiny box within.

It contained a key.

"That's a strange present," remarked Millamant.

Rosamund turned the key over. The back was perfectly flat, as if it had been cut in half right down the middle.

"Is this a joke?" she asked suspiciously. There was no answer. As unexpectedly as she had arrived Madame had departed, and her beige trouser-suit was already beating a retreat into the crowd.

"Charmed, I'm sure," said Millamant. "And to think I sent her an invitation."

"She's seen that key before, Rose," said Emily thoughtfully. "Did you see her face? When you took it out, she looked almost sick. She wasn't expecting it at all. I wonder what it's for?"

"If I need to know, Papa King will tell me," said Rosamund. "As for Madame, good riddance to her. She's not a real relative, anyway." She dropped the key into her diamanté evening bag and snapped it shut.

"Happy birthday, Rosamund!" A group of fans, wearing Minivers T-shirts and badges, emerged from the throng of guests. The Vice-President of the Minivers Fan Club, a young man called Titus, went down on his knees before Rosamund with a bunch of roses. Rosamund smiled as she took the flowers from him and buried her face in their fragrant petals.

"Mmmm. My favourites. Thank you, Titus. You always know just what Emily and I like." She handed the roses to an attendant, who was already holding several huge bunches of flowers. One of the women pushed forward a girl who was about Emily's age.

"Introduce Fiona, Titus, she's new," she said.

"Of course," said Titus, though for a moment Emily thought he did not look pleased. "Rosamund, Emily, this is Fiona Bertram. Her mum, Brenda has just joined our committee."

"How do you do?" Rosamund smiled and reached up to shake Fiona's hand. Fiona blushed furiously. Emily knew exactly what she was thinking. *My goodness, she is so small! I mean, I knew she would be, but she barely comes past my knee. And look at her little hand – why, it's just like a doll's! If I shake it too hard, I'll break it!* Some people were actually rude enough to say things like this to the Minivers' faces, but Fiona had obviously been told how to behave, because she merely asked for an autograph. Rosamund was signing her name with a flourish, taking care to leave room for Emily, when everything went horrendously wrong.

"Of course," Fiona was saying (like a lot of fans, she was trying to sound cool, as if meeting a Miniver was something she did every day), "it's not really your birthday today, is it? I mean, it can't be, if you were found in that shoe box the way everyone says you were. I expect nobody really knows when your real birthday is—"

Rosamund's hand stopped moving over the page. For a moment, her expression froze under her carefully applied make-up. Then her lower lip wobbled. A rush of tears welled up in her big dark eyes, the autograph book fell from her hand, and she fled across the ballroom without another word.

"Rosamund! Rosamund!" Emily dived into the nearest forest of giant adults. As she squeezed out the other side, she knew immediately that everyone had seen. People were turning this way and that, the shockwaves following Rosamund across the crowded ballroom. Rosamund was heading for a side exit, but at the last moment, she seemed to realize she was too small to reach the door handle. She veered, ran up on to the stage where the band was, and vanished through the silver curtains at the back.

Emily hurried after her. "For goodness' sake, start playing!" she hissed to the guitarist as she passed him, for the band had stopped dead and the party had ground to a halt. As she followed Rosamund through the curtains, Emily heard their latest hit start up again behind her, and the terrible sound of Rosamund's weeping ahead.

The backstage area was not large: just a dusty, dimly

lit space draped with black curtains. Emily picked her way carefully over snaking ropes of cable. Rosamund was sitting on a plastic crate, her tiny shoulders convulsed with sobs. She had wrenched the heel off one of her diamanté sandals, and tears were streaming uncontrollably down her face.

Emily knelt beside her. "Rosamund, Rosamund what's the matter?" She reached out her arms and Rosamund clung to her hysterically. Her hot tears flooded over Emily's bare shoulders, and they held each other close.

"Oh, Emmie, I'm so unhappy."

"But Rose, why? She didn't mean any harm. I mean, I don't know when my real birthday is either—"

"Emmie! *Don't!*"

There was the sound of footsteps. Emily glanced up and saw Millamant picking her way towards them. "Please, Rose," said Emily. "Please try and stop crying. You can't storm out of your own party. You have to let the guests know you're all right."

"I'm not all right!" Rosamund wailed. "This is the worst day of my life. Oh, Milly, my face! I must look like a *freak*." And indeed, there was so much eyeshadow and mascara streaming down Rosamund's cheeks that she looked as if she had two black eyes.

"I said you were wearing too much make-up," said Millamant sternly. Rosamund choked and laughed through her sobs. Even Emily managed to smile.

"Why don't I tell everyone you're sick? That you'll be back in a few minutes."

Rosamund shook her head. "I can't go back," she said. "I just can't. Please, Emily. Don't make me. I just want to go home."

Emily looked at her sister's tear-stained face. She still did not understand what was happening, but she knew Rosamund must be really upset to have broken down in front of her fans. "All right," she said. "I'll make an announcement."

Emily walked back to the wings. In the darkness, she unexpectedly bumped into Ron.

"Tell the band to stop playing," Emily ordered him. "Then help Rosamund to the car. You'll need to have it sent to the back entrance so no one sees." She straightened her shoulders. The band was still playing, but at a gesture from Ron, they stopped. The lights in the ballroom dimmed. The guests, who had been milling around, gathered in clumps at the front of the stage.

Emily took a deep breath and walked out on to the stage. The ballroom seemed full of huge sweaty shapes, all staring at her, waiting for her to speak. Cameras flashed and news cameras zoomed in close, but Emily had been appearing on television all her life. She could not remember a time when she had not been in front of one camera or another, and it did not bother her that they were there. The band's guitarist handed Emily a microphone. A spotlight swung down on her tiny figure and she began to speak.

"Tonight is a special time for a very special person. My sister Rosamund is fourteen years old. I'm sure you'd all like to join with me in wishing her a happy birthday." Emily paused, and there was a warm scattering of applause. "Unfortunately, Rosamund has been taken ill. She has had to leave the party and will soon be going home. I know she is disappointed, but it will cheer her up if you can join with me in singing her 'Happy Birthday'."

The band struck up. Emily sang the first phrase into her microphone and, after a ragged start, the crowd warmed up and sang along with her. As she reached the last line, Emily started walking slowly back across the stage. Suddenly, in the midst of the crowd, in front of Rosamund's forgotten birthday cake, her eyes caught sight of Madame. Of everyone in the room, she alone was not singing. She was gazing at Emily with an expression that was almost like hunger it was so intense.

A great fear, unlike anything she had ever felt before, took hold of Emily's heart. The song ended, the spotlight went out. Emily fled the stage while it was still in darkness. The wind of change was in the air, but as yet she had no way of telling in which direction it was blowing.

2
KIDNAPPED

Rosamund was very quiet on the way home. She sat on the back seat of the limousine, surrounded by unopened presents, one hand clasped limply in Emily's. Emily glimpsed a tear on her cheek and tried to speak to her. But Rosamund merely squeezed her fingers and turned her head to stare at the rain-soaked streets.

Lightning flashed, and there were low rumbles of thunder. In the front seats, the driver, Joe, talked about the cricket with Alastair, the duty security guard. Emily wanted to shout at them. Didn't they realize something terrible had happened? Even Millamant, on the opposite seat, had been silent since they left the party. Emily leaned over and whispered in her ear.

"Do you think Rosamund's ill?"

"Shhh." Millamant put a stumpy finger to her lips. Frustrated, Emily picked up a fragrant bunch of red roses, the same colour as Rosamund's dress, and buried her face among the blooms. As she did, a tiny card fell

13

into her lap. *To Rosamund*, it said, *With love from Titus and the Minivers Fan Club.*

The limousine pulled into the driveway of Miniver House. As it slowed in front of the big iron gates, reporters rushed towards them, waving cameras and microphones. Several flung themselves at the car and banged on the doors and windows, while one woman, more agile than the others, landed on the bonnet. She lay spreadeagled for a moment across the windscreen, her mouth opening and closing like a fish against the tinted glass. Emily winced. Joe accelerated through the opening gates and the woman jumped off into the darkness and was left behind.

"I hate it when they do that," said Rosamund, in a muffled voice. "I wish they'd leave me alone."

"She made an awful bump when she hit the bonnet," said Emily anxiously.

"Serve her right if she was run over," said Millamant. "But I don't think she will have been hurt, little Emmie. We were hardly moving. Don't worry, the guards will look after her."

The car pulled up at the terraced front of Miniver House. It was a long, turreted building with two Miniver-sized storeys, painted soft pink and white and nestled about with trees. As soon as the car came to a halt, Rosamund jumped out and ran into the house.

"Rosamund?" Emily hurried after her. The lights were out in the hallway, but upstairs she heard Rosamund's bedroom door slamming shut. Emily turned on the light and followed. She tapped once on Rosamund's door – there was no lock, for they had never wanted to keep each other out – turned the handle, and walked in.

Rosamund was lying on her white and gilt bed. Her face was even paler than normal under her raven hair, and though Millamant had wiped away the worst of the make-up smudges, Emily saw that she had been crying again. She was turning the key Papa King had given her over and over, as if she was standing in front of a door and could not make up her mind whether to open it. The expression on her face was almost more than Emily could bear. She sat down on the bed, twisted her fingers in her lap, then spoke.

"Rosamund, what's the matter?"

Rosamund stopped playing with the key. She looked at it for a moment, put it on the coverlet and propped herself up on her elbow. "Emily, haven't you ever wondered where we come from? I mean, who put me in the shoe box and you in the basket, and why?"

"Sometimes," said Emily slowly. "Well, of course I have. It'd be strange if I hadn't when we look so different to everyone else. But nobody's ever been able to find out the answer to those questions, and if they could, I think by now they would have. Anyway, what does it matter where we come from? Isn't it more important who we are?"

"No." Rosamund sat up suddenly on the bed. "No, it isn't. Don't you understand, Emmie? You and I – we have no real beginning. That's why I got so upset tonight. That girl, Fiona, was right when she said I don't have a real birthday. Neither of us knows when we were born, or where, or even why. Ordinary people, even ones who were adopted, can find the answers to those questions. But you and me – we're not real people at all. We're Minivers. We just – *are*."

"But Minivers belong to everybody," said Emily. It was something Papa King had always told them, and she believed it with all her heart. "Minivers are for people to love."

"Are they, Emmie?" said Rosamund. "Are they really? Papa King taught us that, but since his stroke, I sometimes even wonder about that."

The fear that had been in Emily's heart when she had seen Madame at the party struck her now for a second time. "But the fans love us, Rose," she whispered. "They always have, especially you. Look at the presents and letters people send you every day. You got seventeen sacks of mail this morning just for your birthday. Isn't that enough?"

Rosamund shook her head. "You don't understand. Not now. But you'll know what I mean one day." She shifted restlessly, and the key that Papa King had given her slipped off the bed and landed on the carpet. Emily picked it up.

"Don't lose this, Rose," she said. "It might be important."

"You take care of it for me. You know how careless I am." Rosamund leaned over and kissed Emily on the cheek. "I'm tired, I want to go to bed. Good night, Emmie. Love you."

"I love you too." Emily returned the kiss, and they hugged briefly. But, as she trailed out of Rosamund's bedroom into her own adjoining room, Emily still did not entirely understand.

"Minivers are for everybody." Emily repeated the slogan as she put Rosamund's key in her bedside drawer. Millamant was standing by her bed, turning back the covers and plumping up the pillows. "Minivers are for people to love. Everybody loves the Minivers. Everybody." There was a loud thump on the roof and Emily started. "What was that?"

"It sounded like a possum," said Millamant. She handed Emily her pyjamas. "Is Rosamund all right?"

Emily shook her head. "She says we have no beginning. That being a Miniver isn't enough any more. I don't understand what's wrong with her."

"Growing up," said Millamant wisely. "It was bound to happen, sooner or later. Don't worry, Emmie, she'll be herself again soon enough. Come along to bed." She waited while Emily put on her pyjamas and cleaned her teeth, then tucked her in and left her with a brisk and businesslike kiss.

But Emily could not sleep. She felt stressed and confused, and the evening's events kept running around inside her head. Again and again, she saw Rosamund fleeing across the crowded ballroom, saw Madame's colourless grey eyes staring up at her on the stage. What did Madame mean by walking away like that? What door did Papa King's key open and why had he given it to Rosamund? With all her heart, Emily wished that Papa King was well again. Though he had always been more like a distant grandfather than a real father to her and Rosamund, he had always watched over them and protected them from harm. Emily's eyes filled with tears. The storm was still rumbling and the rain was thrumming on the roof. Once or twice she thought she heard the possums again, going clunk-clunk-clunk over the tiles. Then, at last, without realizing how or when, she fell into a fitful doze.

A shrill, piercing scream brought Emily wide awake in an instant. She sat up, panting and terrified. Her nightie was twisted around her legs and the bedding lay in a heap on the floor. For a moment, she was not sure whether the scream had been real, or whether she had dreamed it. Then she saw something so strange, so almost impossible that for several seconds she sat round-eyed and staring, unable to believe it.

The window was open and the soft plush pink of her bedroom carpet was marked by wet footprints. Somebody had come in through the window, walked through her room in dirty trainers and passed through Rosamund's door, leaving behind bits of wet leaf and mud. And the footprints were normal-sized.

In an instant, Emily was out of bed. She shoved open Rosamund's door and snapped on the light. If Rosamund had been there, she would have screamed and thrown a pillow at Emily's head. But Rosamund was not there. Her Miniver-sized bed, with its gilt bedhead, was empty.

A glass of water had been knocked off the bedside table and the bedding pulled from the bed. As Emily ran to the window and leaned over the sill, a security alarm suddenly went off, shrill, mocking, too late. Dark shapes were running over the lawn of Miniver House. Through the drumming rain, Emily thought she heard a distant scream.

"*Rosamund!*" she yelled.

Now there really was no doubt. Emily turned and ran from the room, stopping only to grab a pair of slippers from the jumble of dresses and miniature feather boas that spilled from her sister's dressing-room. She scurried downstairs, past pictures that showed her and Rosamund together on television, with their gold records, with Papa King. At the bottom of the stairs she bumped into Millamant.

"What's happening?" Millamant's blonde hair stuck out in two stiff plaits on either side of her head. She was in her nightie and had one stumpy arm in and the other out of her dressing gown. "Where's security?"

"I don't know. Milly, somebody's kidnapping Rose! We've got to help!"

"Emily! Emily stay here!" shouted Millamant, but Emily had already wrenched open the door and run out into the rain. Torches were moving through the darkened garden, flickering this way and that; she heard footsteps running on wet gravel and men shouting as the security guards tried to work out which way the intruders were going.

"*Ron! Alastair! What's happening?*" Emily bawled. Ignoring Millamant, who was still yelling at her from the house, she ran across the terrace and down the shallow steps. It was so hard to see anything in the rain and darkness that by the time she reached the bottom she was drenched through and confused about where to go next. Emily hurried over the driveway, her small feet wobbling and stumbling on the gravel. There was thunder in the air and the dim glimmer of lightning. Mist floated across the paths between the flower beds. Emily heard the distant crackle of walkie-talkies, moving around to the front of the house. Then, at the side gate, she heard a car engine starting up in the street.

"*Rosamund!*" Emily darted between two huge pink canna lilies. They shook and rustled over her head as she forced her way through, and she lost a slipper in the sodden mulch as she vaulted from the garden bed on to the grass. Ahead of her, beyond the rose garden, was the murraya hedge that had been planted to keep out prying eyes, and a strong gate that was always secured by a chain. As Emily ran towards it there was a flash of lightning and she saw that the gate was swinging open.

"*Stop!*"

Thunder exploded overhead. In the street, two dark human shapes were wrestling a struggling bundle into the back of a van.

Emily thought she heard a muffled cry. "Rose, I'm coming!" she shouted.

The kidnappers jumped into the van. With a last desperate effort, Emily shot through the gate on to the footpath. As she reached the van, its doors slammed in her face. The driver revved the engine, and it sped off through the teeming streets and was gone.

3

SEPARATION

The morning sun was creeping around the edges of the living-room curtain when Emily was awoken by the sound of a tray being set down on a nearby table. She had been sleeping with her mouth open and it felt dry and horrible. She was tired, as if she had not had a proper night's sleep. For a moment, Emily could not remember why she was lying there. Then she saw Millamant with a pile of newspapers and anxiously sat up.

"Milly! Is there any news?"

"Not yet." Millamant put the papers down. She looked very tired, which was not surprising. They had sat up for hours, waiting for news of Rosamund. Emily had fallen asleep on the sofa some time after dawn, but Millamant seemed not to have slept at all. "I've had the radio and TV on all morning, but there's been nothing on the news reports. Ron says the police want to keep it secret as long as they can, in case it hampers the investigation. He'll be coming in after breakfast to talk to you."

"Oh, Milly." Emily's lip wobbled. "I don't want anything to eat this morning."

"Of course you don't," said Millamant. She picked up the loaded breakfast tray and placed it on Emily's lap. "But I've gone to the trouble of cooking, and you're going to need it. It's going to be a difficult day."

"I suppose so." Emily poked her fork into the middle of her scrambled egg, then put it down on the edge of the plate with a clatter. Tears welled up in her eyes, and she reached for the soggy handkerchief in her dressing gown pocket and started to howl. Millamant's blue eyes watered too. She sat down on the sofa next to Emily and patted her on the back with a small square hand.

"Don't worry, little Emmie. We'll get her back. Rosamund can't be far away."

"She'll be so frightened," wept Emily. "She might be hurt, and, oh Milly, suppose we don't find her? Suppose something terrible has happened? What if – what if Rosamund is *dead*?"

It was the first time she had uttered the word. Millamant looked stricken and had no answer, but Emily could see from her expression that she too, had thought the unthinkable. Their hands fumbled and linked, and for a moment they sat, trying to imagine a world without Rosamund in it, a world so grey and insupportable that neither of them could believe it might exist. The moment was broken by a knock on the living-room door.

"That'll be Ron," said Millamant. "I'll let him in."

Emily pushed aside the untouched tray of food and hastily wiped her eyes. Millamant got up to answer the door.

Miniver House had been designed for Emily and Rosamund, but it had been necessary to cater for normal visitors, too. An average sized person could just about stand up inside if they were careful of things like light-fittings. Ron, the Miniver's Chief of Security, had to stoop to get through the door, and he looked distinctly uncomfortable amongst the miniature furniture. Emily gestured politely to their biggest chair.

"Ron. Please, sit down. I'm sorry, we should have held this meeting in the conference room."

"That's all right, Miss Emily. I'm sure you'll feel more comfortable in your own house. I might kneel, if you don't mind; that chair looks a bit small." Ron crouched down and produced a videotape. "I've brought this for you to look at. It's the edited security footage from the cameras. There's no other news yet, but the patrols are out, and we should get fresh reports within the hour."

"Thank you." Emily put the tape into the video recorder. Black and white, flickering images filled the TV screen. They were so grainy she was unable to make head or tail of them. "What's that?"

"The back roof of the house. If you watch carefully, you should see two intruders coming over the roof, here." Ron slowed the tape so Emily could see more clearly. "This next bit shows them ten minutes later, running across the south lawn – that's probably Rosamund in the sack, over the taller one's shoulder. The next footage comes from the camera outside the gate. You can see them driving off. Does that look like the van you saw?"

"I think so." Emily nodded. "They've got tape or something covering up the number plate."

"That's a pity," said Ron. "The van's a common type. It won't be easy to trace."

"That's the police's job, surely," said Millamant sharply. "Which reminds me: neither Emily nor I have been interviewed yet. I would have thought that should happen as soon as possible."

"I'll ask the detective in charge what he wants to do," said Ron. For a moment, Emily thought he looked annoyed. "I'm keeping him fully informed, of course. My own team's already searching the house and grounds; anything they find will be passed on. As for being interviewed, I can send a member of my own team around to take a statement. What about Primrose?"

"I want to speak to a detective," said Emily. "Primrose is only a security guard. Besides, it's not just a matter of making a statement. I want to offer a reward for Rosamund's safe return."

"Very well," said Ron. "I'll see what I can arrange. Meanwhile, stay indoors and don't speak to anybody. The entire security team's been placed on high alert."

He took his tape and went, leaving Emily with the distinct impression that something very important had been left unsaid.

"That was strange," she said, furrowing her brow. "For a moment there, he was really cross. I wonder why? Of course I need to speak to the police. I want to know what they're doing, and besides, I might be able to help them."

"If you ask me, there's a lot going on that's peculiar," said Millamant, darkly. "Emmie, I have to show you something. I wasn't sure whether I should tell you, because it's not very nice, but I suppose it can't be kept hidden for ever."

She picked up the bundle of newspapers she had put on the table and laid them on Emily's lap. The word *MINIVER* leapt off the front page of the top paper in huge black type, followed by *MADNESS*. For a moment, Emily stared at the words, unable to make sense of them. She unfolded the paper. Her eyes focused on the photograph below the headline and she gasped aloud.

It was a photograph of Rosamund, probably the worst one Emily had ever seen. Her eyes were shut, her mouth was open, and she was running hysterically out of the ballroom of the Artemisia Hotel. Quickly, Emily flicked through the pile of papers. The same photo was on every one, though the headlines were different. *Rosie Lets Rip*, read one. *Has This Miniver Gone Too Far?* said another.

Feeling sick and scared, Emily refolded the papers. "How on earth did this happen?"

"I don't know." Millamant twisted her hands. "I've tried to ring the Miniver Press Office several times, but there's nobody there. It's as if the whole place has just closed down overnight. Emmie, I don't understand. The papers have never published articles like this about you and Rosamund. Papa King doesn't permit it. It just isn't done."

"No," said Emily, shaken. "No, it isn't."

She put the papers down. Of course, bad or embarrassing things occasionally happened to the Minivers, like the day Emily had slipped through a grating and had to be fished out of a smelly drain, or the time the Minivers Make-up Giveaway made girls all over Artemisia come out in blotches. But generally, Papa King made sure the newspapers turned a blind eye to these incidents. Emily had never seen anything as horrible as this before.

"They're all saying Rosamund is a spoiled brat," said Millamant. "There's something else, too. Have you noticed?" She took a newspaper from the pile and let it drop open nearly down to her toes.

Emily pointed to Rosamund's picture. "The photo is the same on every one," she said. "I noticed that, straight away. That means somebody has done this deliberately. Somebody has sent that photograph to the papers and told them exactly what story to write."

"Yes," said Millamant. "A person who wants people to think badly of Rosamund, just at the time she needs help most. Someone in a position of power, who can order the papers to publish something Papa King would never permit if he were well. A woman who hates you and Rosamund and thinks of you as a threat—"

"Madame." Emily could barely say the name. "Oh, Milly, Rosamund was so rude to her at the party. Do you really think. . ." Her voice trailed off. She was aware that many years ago Madame had done something truly terrible. Nobody seemed to know exactly what it was, but she had been sent away from Artemisia by her father, Papa King, never to return. Then Papa King had suffered his stroke, and Madame had come creeping home and moved back into the palace. Ever since her return, all sorts of strange and unsettling things had been happening. Most of them were so small that Emily could not quite put her finger on them. But in recent months the number of newspaper and magazine articles about the Minivers had definitely shrunk, and the people at the palace had become less friendly. It had grown harder, too, for Emily and Rosamund to get news of Papa King, let alone to visit him. Until now, though, it had not occurred to Emily that Madame was behind all of this. In a dim recess of her mind she wondered what would happen if Papa King died. The more she thought about the possibility of Madame becoming queen, the more frightened Emily felt.

"If it really is Madame," she said, in a small voice, "I don't see how we can stop her. The Miniver Press Office reports direct to the palace. And so –" she swallowed, and dropped her voice to a whisper "– so does Ron."

It was a horrible moment. Millamant's face had been very grave: it now turned white. "It would certainly explain why Ron didn't want you to speak to the police," she said in a low voice.

"He really didn't want me to be interviewed, did he?" said Emily. "Oh, Milly, I hope I'm wrong. Ron knows everything about Rosamund and me. I've always trusted him. Do you really think he could have sold us out?"

"There's one way to know for sure," said Millamant.

She went over to the phone, lifted the receiver, and dialled out.

Several seconds passed. Emily sat on the sofa with her legs curled under her, large-eyed with anxious anticipation. Then Millamant spoke.

"Who is this, please? What switchboard? Why wasn't my call put through? That's ridiculous: how can the emergency services number be busy? I want to speak to the police, right now. No, I don't want someone to call me back." She pushed her finger on the speaker-phone button so Emily could hear.

"I'm sorry," a woman's voice was saying. "The number you have dialled is currently unavailable. Perhaps you might like to try again later."

"No, thank you." Millamant hung up. She turned to Emily. "Ever heard of the emergency services number being out of order?" she asked. "This is serious, Emmie. Do you realize what this means?"

Emily nodded. All her life, she had known she was small, but she had never before felt helpless. "It means we're prisoners, just as much as Rosamund," she said. "Only Rosamund's on her own. She's been kidnapped, and no one's even looking for her. By now, she could be anywhere."

"I am a Miniver," Rosamund Miniver told herself, as the van she was travelling in jolted over what seemed to be one speed bump after another. "Minivers are important people. Minivers do not cry. Mess with a Miniver, my friend, and you'll answer for it.

"Do you know who I am? I'm Rosamund Miniver, that's who. *Rosamund Miniver.* I'm beautiful. Everybody says I'm the last word in style and elegance. I have a recording contract and my own line of cosmetics. I'm the star of my own TV show. People name their babies after me. I get over *two hundred* fan letters every day.

"We Minivers might be small," asserted Rosamund, "but we're *tough*." She had been saying this over and over since her capture, but she no longer believed it. Suddenly Rosamund started to cry. She had been tied up in a sack for over twelve hours, and now shut into a suitcase. It was hard to be brave when you couldn't breathe, when every bone and muscle in your body screamed with pain, when your hands were tied, your mouth was gagged; and you were hungry and thirsty and needed to go to the toilet so badly you thought you were going to burst.

"Oh, Emmie, I need you. Where are you, Emmie? Where are you, where are you, *where are you?*"

4

AT WOODLANDS STATION

On the edge of the city, where the suburbs gave out and there were only a few small tumbledown houses and struggling farms, was a forest. Not a real forest. It was more a scrubby wasteland, where local boys went to ride their dirt bikes when their parents weren't around. Most of the time, the only life to be seen was birds and insects. At night it was eerie and abandoned.

About midnight on the night after Rosamund Miniver was kidnapped, a van drove into the bushes with its headlights dimmed. The driver killed the engine. Lit only by its parking lamps, the van coasted rapidly down an almost invisible dirt track and stopped in a clearing at the bottom. The door opened and the driver hopped out. He was young and reasonably tall, but it was hard to see much more, for though it was a warm night, he was wearing dark jeans and a black sweatshirt, with a balaclava covering most of his face.

The driver crunched over stones and twigs to the back door of the van and opened it. He pulled out a jerry can and unscrewed the lid, then splashed liquid over the van's sides and bonnet, in the back, and in the cabin. A strong smell of petrol filled the clearing. The driver tossed the empty jerry can into the back of the van and walked away with a bottle in his hand.

At the edge of the clearing he took a cigarette lighter out of his pocket and lit a wick that was sticking out of the top of the bottle. With one clean, swinging movement, he lobbed it at the van. It hit the side with a satisfying explosion of glass and flame. *Whoomph! Whooosh!* Fire ran over the grass and shot up around the van in fantastic colours of purple, gold and green. There was a crackle and a rush of heat that made the watcher's face glow bright.

The young man watched for a moment, smiling, then turned and started walking away swiftly, back up the hill. He had just reached the road when there was a loud explosion. The ground shook and flames leaped above the trees. Soon, it would all be ablaze and the fire brigade would come to put it out.

By then, there would be nothing left for them to find.

"Really," said Rosamund severely, "this won't do. This won't do at all."

She looked at the woman who was standing sheepishly in front of her. The kidnapper's hands were full of miniature outfits: evening dresses made of gold lamé, ski-pants and jumpers, even a riding outfit. Rosamund folded her arms across her red silk pyjamas. Her mouth was still extremely sore from being gagged, and she was feeling cranky and slightly belligerent. Rosamund did not care. She had just been through the most terrifying twenty-four hours of her life. Being cross helped her feel less frightened and more in control of what was happening to her.

"Dolls' clothes," Rosamund went on, "are for dolls. They are made of cheap, nasty material with no proper fastenings. I am not a doll, and I refuse to wear them. So. What are you going to do about that?"

The kidnapper looked mournfully at the clothes and said nothing. Rosamund gave an exaggerated sigh. The woman's name was Brenda, and in a way, it had been a relief to find that she was just a nutty fan. Rosamund had been afraid – really afraid – that her kidnapper had been Madame. That said, Brenda was definitely one of the weirdest people she had ever met. Her house was weird, too. Wherever Rosamund looked, she saw either her own or Emily's face. The walls were plastered with

Miniver posters, and the floor was stacked with teetering piles of magazines such as *Miniver Matters* and *Minivers Monthly*. There was even dirty Minivers crockery on the table. Rosamund was not very impressed by the standard of Brenda's housekeeping. Millamant would not have put up with it for a moment.

Brenda's daughter, Fiona, sat watching from the sofa under the window. She was a mousy girl of about Emily's age and had so far kept out of Rosamund's way. The third kidnapper had gone out soon after their arrival. Her name was Holly. Rosamund liked her the least of the three, partly because she sensed Holly was not a Minivers fan, and partly because she was the person who had stuffed her into the suitcase.

"Honestly, Brenda," said Rosamund, "the best thing you can do is take me home. You're going to get into a lot of trouble, you know. Oh, for goodness' sake, take those awful things away." As Brenda jumbled the dolls' clothes into a cardboard box, Rosamund's eye fell on a set of display shelves. They were filled with life-size Miniver dolls, including, Rosamund noticed with some annoyance, the really ugly one with the beehive hairdo she had always hated.

She looked them over carefully, then pointed. "There." Standing in pride of place was a limited edition Rosamund doll in a zip-fronted blue velvet pants-suit. "That looks more comfortable. I'll wear that one."

"Oh!" On the sofa, Fiona went white and sat up.

For the first time Brenda showed some sign of emotion. "But it's never been out of the box! There were only three hundred ever made. It'll halve its value!"

Rosamund lifted her eyebrows haughtily. "So?"

Miserably, Brenda shook her head. "I'll get some scissors."

"Good. And while you're at it, you can make me a cup of tea." Rosamund felt a little surge of confidence. "Milk and two sugars. With a biscuit, if you have one. I'm very hungry."

"It says in *Minivers Monthly* you have milk with one," remarked Fiona, as her mother left the room. "I didn't realize you liked your tea with two."

"We don't tell *Minivers Monthly* everything, you know," Rosamund snapped. She looked at Fiona more carefully. "Do I know you? I'm sure I've seen you before, but I can't work out where. Have we met?"

Fiona went bright red. "I don't think so," she said. "I don't go out very often. Please, can I tell you something important? Don't be too hard on my mum. None of this was her idea. She actually thinks – well, other people have persuaded her – that she's doing this to help you."

"Oh, really?"

"Yes." Fiona nodded. "You see, Mum believes she's psychically linked to you. She says she can tell when you're happy and when you're sad. You remember when we had that really bad storm and the big tree fell on Miniver House? Mum says you appeared to her in a dream and told her you and Emily were all right."

"I did?"

"Yes. Well, Mum thinks you did. For a while now, she's been convinced that you're unhappy. She says she can feel you want to get away from everything. I know it's just in her imagination, but Mum believes in it, and it makes her awfully easy to trick."

"Yes, I suppose it would," said Rosamund faintly. She hoped the psychic link was not as strong as it seemed, because at that moment she was thinking the best place for Brenda was the mental hospital. On the other hand, Fiona seemed sympathetic and relatively normal. Rosamund decided to take a gamble. "Fiona, can we be honest? I understand what you're saying about your mother, and I'm not holding it against her, but I need to get out of here. Could you leave me alone, just for a moment? Go and tell your mother I want an extra biscuit or something? If you do, I promise I won't tell anyone she was involved."

Fiona looked Rosamund straight in the eye. With a jolt, Rosamund realized where she had seen her before.

Fiona was the girl who had spoken to her at her birthday party, the one whose embarrassing remark had been the start of everything.

I'll get in awful trouble, Fiona's eyes said to Rosamund. *It's not just my mother. It's the other people you don't know about.*

But if I stay, who knows what will happen to me? Rosamund answered silently. *You know it was wrong to bring me here. I'm in terrible danger, I must get back to my sister.*

There was a strange moment of mutual understanding, and then Fiona said, "I'll be back in a minute."

"Thank you."

Rosamund pressed her hands gratefully together. As soon as she was sure Fiona had gone, she ran to the sofa under the window and vaulted on to it. She had noticed that there was a large hole in the flyscreen, and from the sofa armrest it was easy to climb on to the window sill. Rosamund pushed her head and shoulders through the hole. She pulled herself out on to the outside sill, took a deep breath, and half jumped, half tumbled into the dark, weed-filled garden bed below.

"*Oooff!*" For a moment, Rosamund lay on her back and stared dizzily up at the eaves of the house. Fortunately, the garden bed was soft and damp from the previous night's rain, and she was only momentarily winded. As soon as she recovered, she picked herself up, brushed off her damp pyjamas and, hugging the wall, crept along the side of the house. At the corner, Rosamund paused and looked across the lawn. A dark blue station wagon was turning into the driveway on the other side of the house.

The car was unfamiliar, but Rosamund caught a glimpse of Holly in the front passenger seat and knew it was now or never. As the car disappeared down the driveway, she bolted across the lawn towards the low chain-wire fence at the front of the property. The front gate creaked slightly as she opened it, and then she was running along the footpath for her life.

A long line of wooden houses stretched away in front of her. They were the sort of houses Rosamund had only ever seen on television, with unkempt gardens and old cars, and junk mail poking out of the letter boxes. Rosamund kept as close as possible to the fences, for there was no other cover. Her heart was beating so fast she could almost hear it; she knew that at any moment the door of Brenda's house would open and the pursuit would begin. But though she knew she had to find somewhere to hide, all the gates were closed and the residents fast asleep. There was not a tree on the footpath, and every other garden had a dog that barked ferociously as she passed. Rosamund heard the sound of a car starting up behind her. It screeched out of a driveway and drove off, and she heard angry voices and saw torches flashing over the footpath. Her disappearance had been discovered. The hunt was on.

Too frightened to even think what she was doing, Rosamund dived through a gap in a nearby hedge and flung herself under a parked car. Green eyes flashed like mirrors in the confined space and a cat ran off and jumped over the gate. Rosamund lay as still and quiet as her panting breath would let her. She heard running footsteps and dropped her face into her hands. But the searchers had already gone past. Rosamund waited a moment longer to make sure they weren't coming back, then cautiously crawled out from under the car.

It was clearly too dangerous to go back into the street. Instead, Rosamund stole in the darkness down the side of the house, crossed a backyard with a clothes line, and squeezed through a broken-down fence into a lane. The laneway led past rubbish bins into a larger street. And there, on the opposite side of the road, brightly lit by orange street lamps, was the last thing she had expected to find. It was a railway station.

Rosamund sighed with relief. She had never caught a train in her life, but she had seen people do it in movies and she knew that there would be someone at the station to buy a ticket from. Without a moment's hesitation she hurried across the road, her red pyjamas and painted fingernails showing weirdly black under the amber car-park lights. By now her bare feet were feeling very sore, for she was not used to running without shoes, and her ankles were swollen from being tied up earlier in the day. But Rosamund was not about to give up. She thought of Emily waiting for her back at Miniver House, gritted her teeth, and started to climb the enormous flight of stairs to the station footbridge.

The stairs seemed to go on for ever. By the time she reached the top, Rosamund was breathless and almost crawling. Her feet were filthy and bleeding, and her beautiful pyjamas were covered in dirt, but she pressed on, though limping down the steps on to the platform was, if anything, even harder than climbing up them. Rosamund walked up to the ticket office. To her surprise the shutter on the ticket window was closed.

"Hello?" Her tiny voice wobbled as she called out. There was no reply. Automatic ticket and drink machines whirred under the artificial light and the clock above the platform read 4:27 a.m. Rosamund looked along the platform and noticed a phone booth. Then she glanced across the railway line and saw the kidnappers' dark blue station wagon pulling into the car park.

Rosamund ran to the phone booth. The receiver was

out of reach above her head, and for several useless seconds she jumped frenziedly up and down, trying to reach it. Rosamund grabbed the steel ledge beside the telephone and swung back and forth. Her bare feet scrabbled for purchase on the booth walls and she somehow hooked one foot on to the ledge and hauled herself on to it. Rosamund picked up the receiver. Then she realized that to make a call, she had to put money into the telephone. She, Rosamund Miniver, the richest girl in Artemisia, did not have a penny on her.

"*No!*" Rosamund banged her fist against the keypad. Her eyes fell on a small sign. *Emergency – Freecall – 000*. She leaned over and punched her finger three times against the zero.

There was an unbearable delay while the telephone rang and then a voice said, "Which service, please?"

"This is Rosamund Miniver. This is an emergency! Send the police! No, don't send the police! Put me through to Miniver House immediately!"

"Do you want police, fire brigade or ambulance?"

"You idiot, I said put me through to Miniver House!" yelled Rosamund. "On the palace exchange; it's a priority line. Tell them I've been kidnapped. I'm about to be killed! This is a crisis! They've ambushed me!"

There was a click. For a horrible instant Rosamund thought the woman had hung up. Then, to her unbounded relief, the phone started ringing again. She muttered, "Come on, come on," and suddenly the phone was picked up at the other end and she heard a small familiar voice saying, "Hello?"

"*Emily!*" Rosamund shrieked, and burst into tears. "You've got to help me!"

"Rosamund! Where are you?"

"I'm at the station. The railway station."

"Which railway station?"

"I don't know. How should I know?"

"There'll be a sign, Rose, you have to look." Emily's quiet, patient voice came down the line. "A big sign, it'll be obvious—"

"It isn't there. I can't see it. I don't know where I am." Rosamund looked around frantically, and her eyes fell on a white metal plate with dark red lettering. "Woodlands! It's Woodlands!" she cried, and then the receiver was wrenched from her fingers and Emily, at the other end, heard the line go abruptly dead.

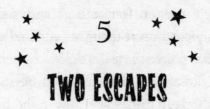

5

TWO ESCAPES

Rough hands dragged Rosamund off the ledge where she was balanced. She screamed and heard the telephone receiver clatter to the ground, then she hit the cement with a jarring thump.

Holly's hands twisted in the collar of her pyjamas and she was dragged out of the phone box. "Thought you'd get away, did you?"

"Let me go!" Rosamund yelled and kicked, but the more she struggled the harder Holly dragged. Rosamund clawed at the woman's wrists with fingernails sharp as needles. Holly jerked at her collar even harder, and suddenly something totally unexpected happened. With a sound of ripping cloth, the whole top part of Rosamund's pyjamas gave way and started sliding up over her head.

Holly made a fruitless snatch at Rosamund's arms and fell over. With a swift twist, Rosamund slid bodily out of her top and ran in her silk singlet and pyjama bottoms across the platform.

"Come back, you idiot!" shouted Holly. "Come back!" She jumped to her feet and started pelting after Rosamund, who was screaming like a steam kettle as she fled barefoot towards the stairs. A loud blare sounded. A train was coming into the station. Rosamund glanced over her shoulder and saw Holly right behind her. Without thinking, she jumped off the platform on to the tracks. She hit the clinker with an agonizing crunch, then flung herself into a roll across the sleepers, landing on the inbound track just as the outbound train came pulling into the station.

For a terrified moment Rosamund lay on the tracks, watching the train go clicking past. There was a sound of brakes and then it stopped. Rosamund realized she had to move. She scrambled to her feet and ran along the tracks towards the back of the train. The train's engine started up again. Rosamund glimpsed Holly between the carriages, running along the platform, and heard a rattling sound on the clinker up ahead.

"Quick! Over here!" A tall dark man was running along the track.

Rosamund ran blindly towards him. "*Help me!*"

In one second, the man had tossed her up over his shoulder like a small sack of potatoes. In another, he had scrambled up the crib wall at the side of the tracks and begun scaling the chain-wire fence that stood on top of it. The whole thing shook and rattled violently. Below her, Rosamund saw the train pulling out of the station, and Holly's furious face looking across the tracks at her and her rescuer. A moment later they reached the top of the fence, and the man who was carrying her jumped to the ground and legged it into the night.

By the time she replaced the receiver, Emily had made up her mind what to do. "Milly, that was Rosamund. She's in trouble. I have to find her."

"What kind of trouble?" Millamant hovered in the bedroom doorway, dressed in her pyjamas. "Where is she?"

"At Woodlands railway station. I don't know what happened, but the call was cut off." Emily hurried into her dressing-room and started pulling clothes determinedly out of drawers.

Millamant followed, a look of dismay on her face. "They'll never let you out! Emmie, we still don't know what this is all about. It's not safe. At least take me with you."

"I can't." Emily pushed in the drawer. "I wish I could, but I need you here to distract Ron and the guards. You know I'm not supposed to go out by myself. If they see me leaving the grounds, they're probably going to try and stop me. And anyway, I don't trust Ron."

"But you'll be all alone!" cried Millamant. "Emily, this is terrible. There must be someone here we can trust."

"Who?" said Emily, and suddenly she felt very small. "There's no one, Milly. No one at all."

Millamant's homely face seemed to sag, and even her stiff little plaits went limp. "Oh, Emmie," she whispered. "Even if we find Rose, what are we going to do?"

"We'll have to worry about that, later." If she stopped to think about it now, Emily knew she would probably burst into tears. "Go and get ready to set off the alarms. That should bring the guards running."

Millamant went. Emily found she was trembling, and tensed her muscles to still them. She pulled on some jeans and a T-shirt and added a pair of boots, and a round hat, to make her feel an inch or two taller. ("Hats are smart," Rosamund had always decreed. "They make even the drabbest person look distinguished.") *Rosamund will need clean clothes, too*, Emily thought, and she crossed into her sister's room and wasted a couple of precious minutes filling a bag with some clothes Rosamund might like to be rescued in. Then Emily realized she had forgotten her car keys. She was scrabbling for them in her bedside table when her fingers unexpectedly encountered a small hard object.

Emily paused. She had forgotten about the half key that Papa King had sent to Rosamund, and that had caused Madame to react so strangely at the party. Her fingers closed around it now, and she took it out and examined it. It looked like a normal house key, though there were more teeth than usual, and one side was ground perfectly flat. Apart from the fact that it had come from Papa King, Emily could see nothing that might make the key important. On impulse, she shoved it into the front pocket of her jeans, slung the bag with Rosamund's clothes over her shoulder, and ran lightly down the stairs to the underground garage.

"I've found the railway station for you." Millamant handed Emily an open street map and pointed to the spot on the page. "Take the motorway, it'll be quickest. I'll go upstairs now and set off the alarms. Good luck, Emmie. Take care."

"Good luck, Milly." Emily flung her arms around Millamant's neck. They embraced so tightly that each could feel the other's beating heart. Then Millamant pulled away. She dropped a kiss on Emily's forehead, nodded briskly, and hurried away.

Emily got into her car and put the key into the ignition. At this moment, she was extremely glad she could drive. Because she and Rosamund were Minivers, and because Papa King was their foster father, they were allowed to do all sorts of things that ordinary girls would never have got away with. Everything inside her normal-sized bubble car had been adapted especially to suit her, from the Miniver-size steering wheel, to the seat with the electric motor that let her see over the dashboard. The brake and accelerator pedals had been especially made for her short legs. Despite this, it was a real car, and could go very fast. Rosamund had one too, but after she'd smashed hers several times, Emily had always done most of their driving.

WAAAAA! WAAAAA! WAAAAA! Even though she had been expecting it, the sound of the alarm made Emily nearly jump out of her skin. She counted a minute by the clock, drew a deep breath, and started the engine. Through the open garage door, she saw the security guards run past along the path above. Emily waited until they disappeared, then revved the car and shot out of the garage with a screech. She hit the gravel in second gear and reached the automatic gates in eleven seconds. The car roared through, the gates closed behind it, and Emily was away.

Emily drove as quickly as she dared for about twenty minutes, then turned off the motorway and found her way through the backstreets to the station. The closer she got to her destination, the more nervous she felt. Saying she was going to rescue Rosamund had sounded fine and brave at Miniver House, but now it was hard to imagine how she would be able to pull that rescue off.

"I am a Miniver," said Emily, under her breath, as she drove into the station car park. "Minivers may be small, but we're tough. I'll think of something." She pulled up in a parking space beside the station footbridge, turned off the engine, and cautiously opened the door.

The car park was deserted, with only a few beaten up old cars parked beneath the orange lights. Emily couldn't see a telephone booth, so she got out of the car, and walked to the foot of the footbridge steps. The size of the enormous flight of stairs made Emily's heart sink, but she started to climb them, and at length reached the top and crossed over to the other side. The station clock showed 5.12 a.m. as she walked down on to the platform. It too was empty, but there was a phone booth near the ticket office, and the receiver had been wrenched off its hook.

A long goods train approached the station and a warm gust of air blew across to where Emily stood. Something fluttered on the edge of the platform, a piece of dark material that lifted and rolled as the train passed, until at length it landed at Emily's feet. She picked it up. The material was so damaged it took her a moment to realize what it was. Then she saw a familiar button and recognized the soft, silky fabric. It was Rosamund's pyjama top.

"*Rosamund.*" A horrible taste flooded Emily's mouth and her hands felt cold against the cloth. There were no bloodstains, but the shirt was torn to shreds and had obviously been under the wheels of a train.

Could Rosamund be dead? Emily was still numbly clutching the pyjama top, when she became aware of someone walking towards her. A tall figure in black jeans was approaching along the platform. Emily looked up with a mixture of suspicion and fear. The young man was wearing a Minivers T-shirt and looked familiar. It was not until he spoke that she realized it was Titus, the Vice-President of the Minivers Fan Club, whom she had last seen at Rosamund's disastrous party.

"Emily? Is that you?"

"Titus!" Relieved that it was somebody she knew, Emily ran to meet him. "What are you doing here?"

"Looking for you, of course." Titus went down on one knee so he could talk to her face to face. "Emily, we had a telephone call from Rosamund at the Minivers Fan Club Headquarters—"

"Rosamund?" cried Emily. "You mean, she's safe?"

Titus nodded. "Of course she is. My friend Holly and I came straight away and collected her. You remember

51

Holly? Dark skin, pretty eyes? She was at Rosamund's birthday party. Rosamund's with her now."

"Thank goodness!" Emily burst into tears of relief. "Oh, Titus, thank you so much! Where's Rosamund now?"

"Holly's taken her back to the Minivers Fan Club Headquarters," said Titus. "Rosamund told us she'd tried to phone you, too, so I stayed behind in case you turned up. I'll take you to her now, if you like."

"That would be wonderful." Emily mopped her eyes with a tissue. "Oh, Titus, this is the best news I've had all day. Just wait until I tell Millamant. She'll be ecstatic."

"You can phone her as soon as we get to the club," Titus promised. "Come on. My car's over there, in the car park. I'll drive you."

"Thank you so much." Emily followed Titus back up the steps and across the footbridge.

His car, a dark blue estate car, was parked in the furthest corner of the car park, and as they walked towards it Titus started talking about the Minivers Fan Club. "Such a shame about Lindsey Smith," Titus said. Lindsey Smith, the club founder and Life President, had recently been very ill. The doctors had never got to the bottom of what was wrong with her, and she had finally left the city to rest up with an aunt. "Still, the club has a great new committee. Over the next few months, we're planning to do a lot of new and exciting things."

"I'm sure you are," said Emily politely, though her mind was on Rosamund, and how soon she would see her. They were crossing the car park to the estate car when she suddenly remembered her own car.

"How silly of me. I forgot, I drove myself here. I'll have to follow you."

"Leave your car here," suggested Titus. "It will be quite safe. You can send somebody to pick it up later."

Emily shook her head. "All the controls are Miniver-sized. An ordinary driver couldn't fit inside." She opened her handbag and searched for her car keys. "Besides, I've got to drive Rosamund. I'll need my car for that. It'll be easier."

"I'm sure the club can arrange something," said Titus. "Honestly, Emily. It's no trouble. No trouble at all."

Emily looked up.

Afterwards, when she tried to think back over what happened, she could not have said what it was that made her do this. Perhaps there had been something just a shade too insistent about Titus's voice, or perhaps her own nerves were on edge, but she instantly knew there was something wrong. Without even thinking what she was doing, Emily reacted. As Titus's hand reached down to grab her, she slung her heavily beaded handbag at his head. It hit with a sickening thwack and flew off into the darkness. At the same moment, the engine of the darkened estate car roared into life.

"Stop her, Holly! Stop her!" Titus lurched towards Emily. She had managed to take her keys out of her bag before she had thrown it at him, and her car was not far away. But Emily's legs were short. By the time she reached the door, there was no time to open it. The estate car was accelerating, bearing down on her. Emily screamed. She flung herself underneath her own car, rolled through the space and emerged on the other side. Titus yelled a horrible swear word, but Emily hardly heard, for at that moment, Holly lost control of the estate car. There was a screech of brakes and a tremendous bang as it ploughed into the bubble car. Emily's car spun around and slammed into a light pole. A second later, the estate car ended under it with a rending crash and was still.

If she had stopped moving for a second, Emily would have been dead; but a survival instinct she had not realized she possessed had stopped her from looking back at the critical moment. When the impact happened, she was on her feet and halfway to the street. She heard a cry behind her, but it was a cry of fury, not of pain. Emily jumped over the car-park wall on to the footpath. A taxi came bearing down around the corner, and she ran out on to the street and flagged it down.

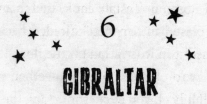

6

GIBRALTAR

"Ow!" yelled Rosamund. Her foot twitched and she wriggled on the edge of the laminated table she was sitting on. "Ow! Ow! *Ow!*"

"Oh, come on," said her rescuer. "It's not *that* bad."

"How do you know?" demanded Rosamund. "It's not *your* foot."

She looked down at her foot where it stuck out beneath the hem of the oversized T-shirt she was wearing. The T-shirt belonged to her rescuer, who was sitting beside her inside what seemed to be a very small, very dingy caravan. He had swarthy skin, a long black ponytail with streaks of grey in it, and a beard and moustache covering most of his face. His jeans were dirty, his boots were down at heel, and his shirt had a rip in it even Millamant couldn't have mended. His name was Gibraltar, and for the last five minutes, he had been watching Rosamund unsuccessfully trying to put a plaster on her cut and bleeding feet.

"They keep sticking together when I take off the paper," said Rosamund. "Oh, look, there's another one gone." The plaster in her fingers folded back on itself, and she tossed it in frustration on the floor.

"Maybe we'd better do it together," Gibraltar suggested. "I'll peel, you stick."

Rosamund looked at him suspiciously. His voice was terribly serious, but the expression on his face made her wonder whether he was laughing at her. Rosamund was not sure what to make of this. Having been famous all her life, she naturally took herself quite seriously, even when she hadn't been kidnapped and nearly flattened by a train. On the other hand, though she would never have admitted it, she had never put on a plaster by herself before. At Miniver House, she had always asked Millamant to help her.

"All right." Rosamund handed Gibraltar the packet and he carefully unpeeled another plaster. Rosamund took it and stuck it on her big toe, which had the worst cut on it. By the time they finished, both her feet were covered with little bits of pink tape.

"Next time you go jumping under a train," said Gibraltar, "make sure you put your shoes on first."

"Thanks for the hint," said Rosamund tartly. She jumped off the bench, curled up her toes and hobbled the length of the van to the door. She had never been in a caravan before, but even to somebody her size, it seemed extremely small. Apart from the table, it contained a tiny stove, two bench seats, and some cupboards. At the far end were two bunks. The bottom one was a bed, while the top bunk was full of papers and books with dark, impressive leather bindings. Everything was neat and orderly and extremely clean. Rosamund, who had had to wash her dirty and bleeding feet in the sink, was very grateful for this fact.

"Well," she said. "Thank you very much for your help, Mr Gibraltar. You came along at a convenient time. But if you don't mind, I'd like to go home now. Do you think you could take me back to town?"

"In a moment," Gibraltar assured her. "You haven't told me what you were doing at the station yet, or why that woman was chasing you. In fact, you haven't even told me your name."

Rosamund stared at him. When Gibraltar had introduced himself, she had not bothered to tell him her name, because she had assumed that he had recognized her. In fact, she had never in her life met a person who had not instantly known who she was. "Do you mean," she said incredulously, "that you don't know me?"

"Should I?" said Gibraltar. "I'm sorry, I didn't realize we'd met before."

"We haven't," said Rosamund. "As a matter of fact, I am Rosamund Miniver."

"Pleased to meet you."

"*Rosamund Miniver*."

"Yes," said Gibraltar politely. "You just said so."

"You've never heard of me," said Rosamund, astounded. She pondered this extraordinary fact for a few seconds, then explained further. "A Miniver is a miniature version of a human being."

"Yes, well, now you mention it, I did think you were a bit undersized," admitted Gibraltar. "Don't worry. Perhaps you'll grow when you get older."

"Grow!" Rosamund drew herself up to her full two feet, three inches. "I am *famous* for being this size. I make CDs. I'm in the papers and on TV all the time. I can't believe you haven't seen me."

"I don't have a TV," said Gibraltar, "and the papers in Artemisia are so full of lies I make it a policy not to believe a word of them. I do listen to records, when I feel like it. That's my gramophone, over there." He pointed to the corner of the caravan, where a record player with a brass horn stood propped up on a milk crate. Rosamund stared in astonishment. She had never seen a gramophone except in very old movies, the sort that were black and white and really boring.

"You must be joking," she said. "You really use that thing?"

"It does work," Gibraltar assured her. "It used to be my granny's. Would you like me to show you?"

"No, thanks," said Rosamund. "You know, you're a very strange person. I can never tell whether or not you're making fun of me."

"Making fun of you? Of course not," said Gibraltar. "As a matter of fact, I've been away from Artemisia for many years. I don't imagine you would have even been born when I left, but I can see quite clearly now that you are famous. You're the sort of girl who naturally would be."

He said this very gravely. Rosamund stared at him for a moment, then saw the twinkle in his eye and burst out laughing. "You are teasing! I knew you were."

"That's much better," said Gibraltar, smiling. "It would be terrible if you really did take yourself that seriously. Now, Miss Rosamund Miniver, jokes aside, you really do owe me some explanations. I'm more than happy to take you home if that's what you want, but you seem to be a girl with dangerous enemies. Before I help you any further, I need to know exactly who they are."

"I'm not sure I can tell you," admitted Rosamund. "It all started the night before last, when I was kidnapped. Holly, that woman at the railway station, was one of the kidnappers. For a while, I thought they were just weird fans, but now I'm not so sure."

"Why not?"

"Well," said Rosamund, "ever since Papa King had his stroke, everything's been very strange. His daughter, Madame, doesn't like my sister and me, but we always thought she was just jealous and nasty. Then funny things started happening. There were a couple of horrible articles about us in the newspapers, and the radio stations stopped playing our latest CD. And then, about two months ago, a lot of our security staff were sacked."

"Sacked?" asked Gibraltar. "By whom?"

"By Ron," said Rosamund. "He's our Chief of Security. He told us the guards had been selling photos behind our backs, but now I think he was just getting rid of them. The kidnappers put me in a sack to stop me seeing, but I could still hear everything they said, and I'm sure one of them was Ron. That's why I want to get back to my sister, Emily. She could be in terrible danger. I was trying to phone her at Miniver House, just before you rescued me."

"Did you get through?"

"Yes." Rosamund shivered. "That's what frightens me. I told Emily to come and get me at the station. Then Holly found me and the call was cut off. Emily's little, even smaller than I am. If Holly waited until she got to the station, she might try to kidnap her instead of me."

"You don't know Emily went to the station," Gibraltar pointed out. "She might have sent somebody else to find you."

Rosamund shook her head. "She wouldn't. I know she wouldn't. No matter how many fans we have, Emily and I love each other far, far more. We're Minivers you see, the only Minivers alive. If Emily was kidnapped, I'd give everything to get her back. I'd steal, I'd lie, I'd fight, and if I had to, I'd die. And Emily would do the same for me. That's why it's so important I go back to Miniver House. I have to make sure she's safe."

"I can see why you want to do that," said Gibraltar. "But I think it would be very ill-advised. If what you've told me about your security team is right, you'd be walking straight back into the hands of the people who kidnapped you in the first place. Tell me: you mentioned Papa King. Do you know him well?"

"Yes," said Rosamund, surprised by the question. "Emily and I are his foster daughters."

"Ah," said Gibraltar, nodding. "So that's why Madame doesn't like you." He saw Rosamund looking curiously at him, and smiled. "Now you're wondering whether I know Madame. I did meet her once, a long

61

time ago. I used to know your foster father quite well, though I haven't seen him in many years."

Rosamund seized on this. "You were a friend of Papa King?"

"No," said Gibraltar. "I said I knew him. We disagreed about many things. But he always trusted me, and because of that, I promise I will be a friend to you."

Rosamund looked up at him for a moment, uncertain what to say. She knew that Papa King had rarely trusted anyone. But there was something in Gibraltar's eyes that told her he was the sort of person who would speak what he knew to be the truth, no matter what the consequences.

She said, "Why should I trust you? I never met you until this morning. How do I even know you'll do what you say?"

"Because I rescued you when you were in trouble," said Gibraltar. "And by now, I think it's quite likely I'm the only friend you have."

The morning traffic was building as Emily headed back along the motorway to Miniver House. From low down in the back seat of her taxi, she watched the familiar silhouette of the city buildings drawing closer. The cranes on the skyscrapers pointed at the clouds like fishing rods. On Observatory Point the weather beacon showed a clear day ahead.

"I can't get over this," said the cabbie. His name was Kevin, and when Emily had first flagged him down he had been dumbstruck. But he had accepted her story about being involved in a car crash, and was thoroughly enjoying driving his celebrated passenger home. "My daughters are going be so excited when I tell them who was in my cab. Would you mind giving them your autograph?"

"Of course," said Emily mechanically. Normally she would have promised to send a photograph, but just now she felt so tired and bruised on the inside by all that had happened, that she could scarcely talk. The taxi glided on to an off-ramp. A line of cars had formed a traffic jam along the approach to Miniver Boulevard, and as the taxi inched off the motorway they suddenly found themselves surrounded, not just by cars, but by people.

"That's strange," said Kevin. "I wonder if there's been an accident?"

Emily sat up and craned her head so she could see better. The traffic was gridlocked all the way along the street, and the people on the road and footpaths were all walking purposefully in the same direction. The crowd was so big it had spilled off the pavements on to the street, and was blocking the flow of traffic.

"What's happening?" Kevin automatically turned up the volume on his two-way radio. A crackly succession of voices came over the airwaves.

Emily heard the word "Minivers", followed by something else she could not understand.

"What did they say?"

"It sounds like there's some kind of demonstration outside Miniver House," said Kevin, who was more experienced than Emily at picking up what the operator was saying. "I wonder if there's something on the ordinary radio—"

"No!" Convinced something was very wrong, Emily leaned forward. "Stop here. I have to get out, now. I have to find out what's happening."

"Well, we're not going anywhere else," said Kevin sensibly. "But you can't go alone through that mob. You'll be trampled. Wait while I park the cab."

He pulled out of the line of traffic and stopped under a NO STANDING sign. As soon as he parked, he pulled a cardboard sign out of the glovebox and propped it up on the dashboard. It said RUN OUT OF PETROL. "That should keep us out of trouble for the moment." Kevin rummaged on the floor and passed a greasy tartan rug over into the back seat. "Wrap that around your head and shoulders. It might be best if nobody sees you."

Emily nodded. Kevin got out of the car, opened her

door, and swung Emily up into his arms like a baby. He tucked the rug around her legs to hide her jeans and strode away to join the marching crowd.

There were a lot of police about, both on foot, and on horseback, and Emily counted half a dozen patrol cars and police vans. A huge protest seemed to be in progress outside Miniver House, and people were pressed up against the main gates. Anxiously, Emily pulled the rug up around her face. She thought she had never before heard so many angry voices, shouting and chanting over and over. *We want Rosamund. Give us Rosamund. We want Rosamund. Show us Rosamund.*

Emily felt Kevin grip her more tightly. Step by step, he pressed on determinedly through the crowd. Since he didn't seem to care about pushing and shoving and squashing other people's toes, it didn't take them long to reach the front.

The footpath outside Miniver House was lined with police and security guards. Mounted police patrolled, back and forth, and there was a constant click and snap of walkie-talkies. Something was happening outside the house, but it was too far away for Emily to see exactly what. The waiting crowd grew more and more restless, shuffling its feet and pushing against the line of police as more people arrived at the back.

Finally, from the other side of the gate came the low

sound of a car engine, and wheels crunching over the gravel drive. The automatic gates slowly opened and a police van came out. As it drove through the cordon of police, Emily saw a small frightened figure huddled in the back, flanked by two grim-looking policewomen.

"*Millamant!*"

Emily's scream was drowned by a shriek of hatred from the crowd. Tins and bottles and rotten fruit started flying through the air and the crowd surged forward, yelling and jeering. "Murderer! Murderer! Give us Rosamund! What have you done with her?"

"It's a mistake! Stop! Let her go!" Emily threw off the blanket and wriggled furiously in Kevin's arms. He lost his grip and she dropped to the ground, disappearing at once into a forest of legs. "Rosamund's not dead!" Emily shouted. "You're wrong! Oh, Millamant! Milly! I'm *here!*"

"Hey! Come back!" Kevin fought towards her. He gave a great cry, that was suddenly cut off. Emily jerked her head back. Two Minivers security guards had emerged from the crowd and grabbed Kevin from behind. She saw them dragging him off; then looked forward, and saw Millamant being driven away in the police van.

Panic seized Emily and she began to run. A few people saw her, or thought they did. Some of them grabbed at Emily as she forced her way between their legs, but she was too low down, and the crowd was too dense for them to catch her. Emily thrust her hands into her jeans pocket, found her car keys, and hit the opener for the automatic gate. It began to rattle open again, and before anyone realized what was happening, she shot out of the crowd and sprinted through it, hitting the close button as she went.

"Help! Help!" Emily shouted. She had done what anyone would do in a crisis, and run for home, but the moment she hit the wide expanse of lawn, she realized her mistake. The grounds of Miniver House were alive with security guards. Several of them saw her at once and took up the pursuit. Emily changed direction. She ran for the shrubbery, where the bushes pressed low against the ground and the guards could not easily follow. Emily dived into a clump of azaleas. Their twiggy branches scraped her face and arms as she forced her way through, but the undergrowth was too thick for her pursuers to see exactly where she had gone. When she reached the middle of the shrubs, she stopped. If she was still . . . very still. . .

"She's gone into the bushes!"

"Is that her there? Look!"

Emily crouched as quietly as possible, mentally kicking herself for wearing a white T-shirt and hoping the sound of her breathing wouldn't give her away. The guards blundered around in the bushes for a while, then their voices faded. They had switched their search to the other side of the shrubbery.

Emily crawled away through the mulch on her hands and knees. It was hard to be completely sure where she was going, and impossible to move without making noise, but at last the twiggy undergrowth ended. Emily waited under a bush. A minute or two went past, and she decided it was safe enough to venture out.

She emerged on to a terraced flower bed that sloped down in shallow steps to a sunken pond full of goldfish and waterlilies. In summer, it was one of Emily's favourite spots in the whole garden; she loved to walk on the Miniver-sized brick path that ringed the pool, and sit among the sheltering ferns and feed the fish. Without any clear idea of what she was doing, Emily picked her way down the shallow terraces to the path. She had just reached the last step when a woman's voice unexpectedly shouted, "There she is!"

Emily gasped. Two guards – Emily recognized Primrose and Alastair – came crashing out of the trees on the other side of the pond. Emily jumped off the terrace on to the path.

"Cut her off! Quick!"

Emily veered back in a panic, took a running leap, and flung herself into the pond. It was shallow, but deep enough for a Miniver to swim in, and she dived under the waterlilies in what she hoped was the right direction. She surfaced at the end of the pond, where a rockery filled with ferns overhung the water. In the middle of the rocks was a dark opening. It was a sort of culvert, leading to an overflow pipe that drained away excess water in heavy rain. And it was just big enough for Emily to squeeze into.

Emily hauled herself out of the water and slid without hesitation into the stinking pipe. It was full of horrible, slimy mud that made her slip and slide, but she kept going as quickly as she could on her hands and knees. Behind her, she heard Alastair and Primrose splashing through the pond. Their torches flicked on and focused on the spot where Emily had disappeared.

"She's gone into that drain," said Alastair.

"She won't get far." Primrose stopped in satisfaction at the mouth of the pipe and shone her torch down the narrow passage. Something moved inside, and then was still. "Look. She's jammed up against a grille about three or four metres in. It must be have been put in to keep out animals." A flare of static sounded on Primrose's walkie-talkie and she lifted it triumphantly to her mouth. "Is that you, sir? Emergency over. We've got her."

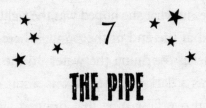

THE PIPE

On a bend in the river not far from Papa King's palace and Miniver House, stood a strange building. It was set apart from its neighbours, in the middle of a stone courtyard, and had no windows in any of its four stone walls. Its double bronze doors were surrounded by a glistening mosaic that shone in the sun by day, and by the light of the street lamps at night. They were guarded around the clock by security guards with guns, though whether they were there to keep people out or in, no one could say.

The building contained the City Archives. Every morning, around six o'clock, the first person to arrive was Livia Wallace. Livia had work she needed to do before the rest of the staff turned up, and if she got there early, she had the building to herself for an hour and a half. This morning, as she nosed her little yellow car into its usual parking spot, Livia was very late and a trifle flustered, for she had spent two hours stuck in a traffic jam. The radio had said something about the Miniver sisters, but Livia had no interest in Emily and Rosamund, and had turned it off. She lived in her own world of files and papers and secrets, and this morning she had much more important things to worry about.

"Morning." Livia flashed her pass at the security guards. One of them pulled out his enormous bunch of keys to unlock the doors, and she passed mechanically under the shining mural into the archives foyer.

The phone call from Madame had come in very early that morning. In fact, it had woken Livia up in her hammock on the verandah, and she had come tumbling inside in such a hurry she had kicked over the milk bottles. "You must speed up the search, Livia," Madame had whispered urgently down the phone. "Things are happening so quickly, I can't hold them back. I'm doing everything I can to find the key, but I haven't been able to get it yet. You understand, don't you? If you don't find that room quickly, it could all still go wrong."

"I understand," Livia had answered. Her bare toes curled up off the wooden floor, and she brushed a loose strand of hair off her cheek. "Only – it's a big place. I can only do so much without people noticing—"

"I don't want your excuses, Livia." Madame's voice was suddenly sharp. "You said you'd help me. I'm relying on you."

"I'm sorry." Livia's fingers twisted in the telephone cord. "Of course, I promise, I'll do whatever I can."

"You're so kind to me, Livvy," said Madame pathetically. "So kind. I sometimes think you're the only one who cares about me at all."

"You're my cousin, Karen," Livia had said, and it was true. Although Madame was a lot older than she was, her mother, Susan, had been Livia's mother's older sister. "Of course I care about you. Don't worry. I'll get dressed and go in right away."

The bronze doors closed behind Livia's back, shutting out the sunlight. Livia drew a deep breath, and headed for the stairs that led down to the stacks.

The City Archives collected paper. If you were born or married or died, if you owned a dog, or bought a house, or did anything at all, it was there, locked away on nine floors of dingily lit basements that reached below the level of the Artemisia River. The deeper down, the danker and more airless the basements got. Most of the files were never looked at, and many had mouldered almost to nothing. But there were some files that were so important or dangerous that nobody except Papa King was allowed to see them. These secret files were locked away in a Most Secret Room, somewhere in the very heart of the building – only now that Papa King was ill, nobody was exactly sure where it was.

72

It was this room that Livia was trying to find for her cousin Karen. She had been searching for months, without success. Livia had looked for hidden spaces in almost every room on the upper levels, and was currently mapping and measuring in the second bottom basement, a place where nobody went unless they absolutely had to. The eighth basement was infested with rats and giant cockroaches that filled the records with droppings. It was so bad there, that when somebody wanted a file, the archive porters drew straws to choose the person who had to do it. But even the eighth basement was not as bad as the ninth. No one, absolutely no one, went to the ninth basement of the City Archives. It was simply too horrible to be spoken of.

Livia made her way down flight after flight of badly lit stairs. She passed the land records and the probate section, and continued on through Education and Public Works. At the top of the eighth flight of stairs she paused. A horrible smell rose up from the darkness to meet her; the smell of long years and decayed paper, of thousands upon thousands of forgotten lives. It was the smell of Artemisia. Livia closed her eyes briefly. She reminded herself of how poor Cousin Karen had been sent away for doing nothing at all, how she had been treated so unfairly by Papa King that her life had been ruined for ever. She thought of how Karen had come back to Artemisia and needed Livia's help. Livia opened her eyes. She switched on her torch, gripped her tape measure, and slowly began to descend the metal stairs.

Inside the pipe, Emily sat panting and shaking in a trickle of dirty water. There was a lot of activity outside in the pond, and she could hear Primrose and Alastair talking on their radios. From time to time arms or torches were poked into the opening, but her tormentors could not reach her. The fact was small consolation to Emily. A metal grating blocked the pipe at her back. If the guards could not get in, she could not get out.

Finally, a voice Emily recognized called her name. It was Ron.

"Emily? Emily, what are you doing?"

A torch flashed into the opening. Emily whimpered and hid her eyes, but the torchlight raked over her body and stayed there. Ron's face, with its thatch of sandy hair, appeared like a hideous gargoyle at the pipe's end. When he spoke, it was in the sort of coaxing voice he might have used to call a lost dog. "Emily. Come out, Emily. Please, come out."

"Get lost!" Emily's voice sounded small and wobbly. "Leave me alone!"

"You're being silly, Emily. You can't stay down there. It's not safe. We're your security team. We're here to look after you."

"You've got a funny way of doing it."

"Come out, Emily," Ron repeated. This time, he did not sound quite so polite. "You know you're trapped. I can set a round-the-clock watch on you. There's no way out."

"Go away!"

The torch flicked off. Emily heard the guards talking. "She's not going to come out," said one of them. Emily thought it might have been Alastair. "She knows something's up. She was always the one with brains."

"If she won't come out of her own accord," said Ron, "then we'll have to make her change her mind. Try this."

There was a scraping noise at the entrance to the pipe. A broken rake with a fan of sharp metal tines thrust into the opening and wriggled violently around. Emily screamed and recoiled against the grating. To her surprise, it shifted a little under her weight. The rake thrust vainly back and forth a few more times, then disappeared.

"She's too far back, sir," reported Primrose. "I can't reach her."

"We could hose her out, I suppose," said Ron. "One

of those big high-pressure hoses would do the trick. Or a smoke bomb, if we could get one quickly."

"We'd have to be careful," said Alastair dubiously. "We don't want her to drown or suffocate."

"What about the rat patrol?" asked Primrose. Emily shuddered. The rat patrol was a pack of horrible little dogs trained to hunt rats out of buildings. They chased the creatures into every sort of nook and cranny and shook them by the head to break their necks.

Fortunately, Ron seemed to like the idea as little as Emily did. "No," he said. "I think that would be overdoing things. Go and get the high-pressure hose, Primrose, and be quick about it. Alastair, you wait here to make sure she doesn't go anywhere. Put that rock across the entrance to keep her trapped in the pipe. I'm going to report to the palace."

Ron and Primrose waded away and climbed out of the pond.

Alastair set his torch down on a boulder. He picked up the rock Ron had indicated, and was starting to shove it into the end of the pipe when he was interrupted by a shrill cry.

"Don't shut me in! Please, don't shut me in!"

Alastair stopped. For a moment he balanced the rock against the edge of the pipe, and then he set it aside and shone his torch into the opening. A tiny abject figure in a bedraggled T-shirt and jeans was sitting hunched up against a grating about three or four metres in. Its face was filthy and wet with tears. Alastair had known to expect this, but he had been with Emily and Rosamund for several years and had seen them many times at their glamorous best. Despite himself, he was shocked.

"I'm sorry, Miss. I don't really have any choice," he said. "The boss told me I had to do it. It'd be more than my job's worth not to."

"It's dark in here," wailed a small voice. "I'm scared of the dark. You know I'm scared. Please don't shut me in here without a light!"

"You could always come out," Alastair pointed out.

"I can't. Please, Alastair. At least give me the torch. You know I'm only little. I'm so frightened!"

Alastair hesitated. He had never heard Emily complain about being small before. On the other hand, the thought of what was happening to her made him feel extremely uncomfortable. Alastair did not understand what Ron and the others were up to, but he was a decent man and knew in his heart the explanations he had been given were a sham.

"All right. I suppose you can have my torch." Alastair turned it off and pushed it as far as he could down the pipe with the broken rake. A few seconds passed, and then a faint glow shone out from between the rocks.

"Got it. Thank you. Thank you so much."

"You're welcome, Miss Emily," said Alastair, and he reluctantly blocked the mouth of the pipe with the stone.

Emily turned on the torch. She could not believe her luck, for she had been sure Alastair would not fall for her claim to be afraid of the dark. But then, he had always been nice to her. Perhaps he had simply been sorry. As she shone the torch over the surrounding pipework, Emily saw for the first time that it was made of long straight terracotta sections. Everything was caked with filth, but when the light flashed over the metal grating at her back, it was all she could do to stop from crowing. Her suspicions had been right. The metal was old and badly rusted, and the pipe around it was cracked in several places.

Emily put down the torch and scraped away the rubbish. At first she was uncertain whether it would be better to push or pull, but after a moment's thought she sat down, braced herself with her hands, and kicked out with all her might. The grating did not give way and the noise she was making sounded horribly loud in the confined space. After a few more kicks, the terracotta crumbled and the metal broke free. Emily got up and leaned against the grating with all her weight. The pipe cracked, the grating collapsed and she half fell, half stumbled through to the other side.

The pipe ahead was made of the same sort of terracotta, badly damaged, with a trickle of sludgy water in the bottom. It seemed to go for quite a distance. Emily had no idea where it went, but there was no other way out. Luckily the torch was a good one, and she hoped the batteries were new. She pushed the grating roughly back into place behind her and hurried forward, sensing as she did that the pipe was sloping gently downwards. The further she went, the more horrible it became. Festoons of roots hung through the cracks in the roof of the pipe and brushed against her head and shoulders, and the cockroaches and beetles that ran from her torchlight grew bigger with every step forward. Worst of all, the further she got from the entrance, the more it stank.

Emily began to feel sick and dizzy. The air was foul, her back ached from the constant stooping, and from time to time her foot stuck in a broken bit of pipe, or squelched in some particularly sludgy patch she preferred not to identify. It seemed as if she had been walking in the darkness for ever when something completely unexpected happened. The pipe came to a join and forked in two.

"Oh, no." Emily slumped into a miserable squat against the wall and began to sob. Ever since she had started her journey down the pipe, part of her had been wondering whether it was a wise thing to do. Now, she wished the idea had never entered her head.

I'm going to die, she thought. *Who knows where this pipe will end up? They're going to put that hose in the entrance, or else they'll send a dog after me, and I'll be killed. That's what they want, I'm sure. And I'll never even get to know what this is all about.*

Well, that's a fine way to think, said Millamant's familiar voice inside her head. *I never thought you'd give up so easily, Emmie. Use your brains: what goes in must come out, you know.*

At the thought of Millamant, Emily's tears streamed even harder. Eventually she managed to mop her face with the end of her T-shirt and shine her torch first one way, and then the other. The pipe on her left sloped up and she realized it must come from Miniver House. There was no point in going that way. Ron would certainly have posted guards there, and with Millamant arrested, there would be nobody left to help her. The right-hand fork continued downwards. It was darker and smellier, but Emily realized she had no choice save to follow it.

Emily forced herself to start walking. Her torch,

which was designed for an ordinary sized adult, was getting heavy, and a few minutes further along she found a dead rat, bloated and horrible, jammed against the wall. It smelled so bad Emily had to hold her nose to stop from throwing up as she passed it. The downward slope seemed to be getting steeper, and the water grew deeper. Before long Emily had to wade. What would she do if the pipe came out underwater? Suppose she ended up in the sewer, and was attacked by rats? The batteries in the torch were running down. If her light went out, she would be trapped for ever in the darkness, until she died or went mad, or starved. . .

And then, when she had almost given up, Emily saw it. There was light ahead, and another grating. Emily began wading more quickly. As she neared the grating, she found she could turn off the torch and see by daylight. The grating was cracked and broken like the first one: a swift kick smashed it open, and then Emily was out in the open, standing in the sunlight she had thought she would never see again, alone on the muddy banks of the Artemisia River.

In a shabby office in a corner of the royal palace, Madame was waiting for a telephone call. She had not slept properly for two whole nights, and was drinking a cup of coffee to try and keep herself awake. It was watery coffee, because that was the only sort Madame made. In fact, if somebody had given her coffee that was properly made, she would probably have thought it tasted very nasty indeed.

Madame was thinking about Rosamund Miniver, and what she was going to do with her. It was a subject she found eternally fascinating. In her heart, Madame was convinced that Rosamund had stolen her place in Papa King's affections, and that it was because of her and Emily that she had been sent away. In fact, Madame and her mother had been exiled for a very good reason before Rosamund was even born, but like most evil people, she was reluctant to accept that she had done anything wrong. Sometimes, at night in bed, Madame used to make believe she had killed Rosamund Miniver and taken her place. She would stab her, or poison her, or drown her, and when Rosamund begged for mercy she would laugh and strike her down. So strong and powerful were these dreams, and so real, that Madame would often forget who she really was and become, in some strange way, Rosamund Miniver herself. In her dreams, she would become beautiful, rich and famous, and people everywhere would love her. They would cheer at the sound of her voice, and tremble with excitement at the very mention of her name.

For many years Madame's dreams had remained just that: dreams. Then two things happened that changed everything. First, Madame's mother died. And gradually, it became known that, following his stroke, Papa King was completely helpless. Madame had seized her chance. She had gone home to Artemisia and moved into the palace. Her plans to become queen had been progressing nicely, and she had been almost ready to move when Papa King had ruined everything by giving Rosamund Miniver the key.

Madame had panicked. The key, so seemingly unimportant, was essential to her plans. She had ordered Rosamund to be kidnapped, and immediately everything had started to go wrong. Madame was desperate. She had to know where the key was. She had to get the Miniver sisters back. . .

The telephone rang. Madame picked up the receiver and listened in mounting anger to the person at the other end. "This is all your fault," she said in a cold voice. "I'm not interested in your excuses. Do whatever you have to, but find those girls. I'd prefer them to be alive, but dead will do. No, I don't want to hear about your injuries. Just get me the Miniver sisters, and everything will be all right."

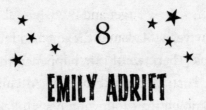

8

EMILY ADRIFT

Black Monday.

Afterwards, whenever people in Artemisia referred to the day on which they learned the Minivers had gone missing, this was the name by which it was called. It was the day Artemisia changed for ever, when the golden legend of the Miniver sisters came to an abrupt and ugly finish. Black Monday was the end of an era. Even the most dull-witted citizen realized the fact, though at the time, the real nature of the change was not yet fully understood.

The official announcement was made on the news at midday. A spokeswoman from the palace confirmed that the Minivers were missing, believed kidnapped. Mr Ron Burgess, the Minivers' Chief of Security, refused to comment on whether the abduction was an inside job. By then, rumours had been flying around for hours, and there were few Artemisians who had not heard some garbled version of what was happening. Crowds had been milling around the gates of Miniver House since before dawn; as hope faded, and the rumours were confirmed, they grew larger and more tearful. The worst was whispered: that Rosamund was certainly dead, that a ransom had been demanded for Emily, that both sisters had been smuggled out of Artemisia to an unknown location.

Newspapers printed edition after edition, and every one sold out as soon as it hit the streets. In school playgrounds, children pooled their lunch money to pay Emily's ransom, and even the crime rate dropped as burglars stayed home to watch the news. Boy scouts and girl guides organized search parties in local forests. One group found a mysterious burned-out van, but the scout leader told the children it was just a stolen car that somebody had dumped. At Miniver House, the switchboard was jammed with calls from people wanting to help.

By Monday evening, Artemisia had almost ground to a halt. The gates of Miniver House had become the scene of a candle-lit vigil, where thousands of devoted fans gathered to lay flowers, sing Minivers songs and wait forlornly for the sisters' return. But though the carpet of cellophane-wrapped flowers began to spread across the footpath, there was still no real news. Rosamund and Emily were gone, and the iron gates of Miniver House remained resolutely shut.

Tuesday morning dawned over the river bright and clear. It was going to be a hot day, for the summer weather had arrived, and there was no cool breeze to stir the leaves of the trees in the river parklands. The water reflected the bridge and city buildings like a mirror, though from time to time the wake of a passing boat rippled over and spoiled the picture.

There was more traffic on the river than was usual for this time of day. A boat full of divers had anchored behind Miniver House and a big blue police launch had already gone up and down several times. Every time the launch went past, it rocked a cluster of yachts moored in the bend of the river. There were nine or ten of them, and from one of the portholes in the smallest one, a tiny pale face might be glimpsed peeping out.

The yacht was called *Bella-Mae*. Emily had swum out to it on the previous morning, after her escape from the pipe, before the search had turned to the river banks, and the sniffer dogs had been brought in to track her down. The effort of reaching the boat had nearly killed her. Emily had always been a good swimmer, but the yachts were moored further out than they looked from the river bank, and by the time she found an open hatch on *Bella-Mae*, she had been so exhausted it was all she could do to crawl into the cabin and collapse. Here she had slept for over fourteen hours, awaking in pitch darkness with stiff limbs, a headache, and no idea where she was.

It had been a terrible awakening. Emily had sat on her bunk and cried until she felt she was going to turn herself inside out. Never in her life had she felt so alone. What was happening was so unreal she could not even begin to comprehend it. From the moment she had been left in the basket, with her name on a label tied to her wrist, Emily had lived to be adored. Minivers were for people to love. That people might treat her harshly, that the glorious, wonderful Miniver existence should ever come under attack, and worst of all, that anyone would ever separate her from Rosamund, had simply never occurred to her. It was as unthinkable as the sun falling out of the sky and crashing into the sea.

I should never have run away, she thought self-pityingly. *What was the point? They're going to catch me eventually, anyway. At least if I'd gone with them, I'd be with Rosamund.*

But Rosamund wasn't their prisoner, Emily's sensible streak reminded her. *She'd escaped, remember? Maybe they didn't recapture her. Maybe she's free, and you can find her.*

I can't, wept miserable Emily. *I'm frightened. I'm lonely.*

I want to go home. But even when her heart was breaking, Emily was too practical to cry for ever. As the dreadful hours of the night had at length given way to the morning she had determined to do something. Emily had climbed out of the bunk and blundered around in the semi-darkness until she found a toilet and a tap to drink from. The water had been stored in plastic tanks in the bottom of the boat and was not very nice, and it was hard work pumping the little handle on the side of the tap. But Emily was so thirsty she did not care, and when she had finished drinking, she filled the sink and washed her face and hands until she felt refreshed.

They won't find me, she comforted herself, as she sat by the porthole, watching the police launch. *They'll be searching along the river banks. No one will think of looking in the boats.* Emily knew this was not true, but she was also aware that she could not sail *Bella-Mae* by herself, or swim away without somebody seeing her. Having chosen a boat for a hiding place, she had no option but to make the best of it until nightfall.

And really, Emily decided as she looked around, *Bella-Mae* was a very nice place to hide. It was neatly fitted out with a bunk in the prow, a table and benches, and a galley space with a stove for making meals. Best of all, the galley locker contained tins of food, crackers (rather stale, but not too horrible), a packet of rubbery cheese in aluminium foil, and breakfast cereal in an unopened box. There was even milk in long-life containers. It was not very exciting food, but there was enough there for someone as small as Emily to live on comfortably for several days. After all she had been through, just the idea of being able to eat breakfast immediately made Emily feel more cheerful.

As long as the owners don't come back, thought Emily, as she poured herself milk and cereal, *I can hide here as long as I like. There are magazines and books. Why, there's even a radio and a little television. It'll be just like my own secret hideout. I wonder why Rosamund and I never thought of buying a boat of our own? It would be such fun to go sailing around the bay, all by ourselves. . .* This was such a nice thought that, by the time she finished her second bowl of cereal, Emily was almost smiling. She stood on a tackle box to fill the sink and wash her cup and breakfast bowl, then went looking amongst the owners' things for something clean to wear.

Her own jeans and T-shirt were filthy. Emily doubted they would ever recover from her experiences in the pipe, but she knew Miniver-sized clothes might not be easy to come by in future. She put on a woman's shirt she found, hung Rosamund's key around her neck on a piece of string and endeavoured to wash her things. It was extremely hard work, especially as she had never done it before, and her hands were far too small to wring things out properly. But Emily did her best, and when she finished, she draped her wet washing proudly over the kitchen bench to dry.

"Now let's find out what's really going on," said Emily, and she climbed up on to the table and switched on the television. She had already found a bank of switches that controlled the yacht's power supply, and was starting to feel more comfortable in her new surroundings. It was obvious, of course, that what was happening to her and Rosamund would be in every newspaper and on every radio and television station in Artemisia. Nevertheless, the face that appeared on the TV screen was not at all what Emily was expecting.

"*Madame!*" A wave of such fear and revulsion swept over Emily that it was all she could do not to turn the TV off. Madame was dressed in a grey suit, with a small white rose pinned to the collar. Like all her clothes, it did not suit her much, but it was obvious she had made an effort to look nice, for she was actually wearing make-up. She was staring at the camera with an earnest expression and talking in a strange voice that Emily guessed was her attempt at sounding posh.

"Papa King and I would like to thank everyone for their immense kindness and sympathy," Madame was saying. "This is a terrible time for us both. But we would like to assure you all that everything that can be done is being done, and I will *personally* ensure that no stone is left unturned in our search to find dearest Rosamund and Emily—"

"Dearest!" cried Emily. "*Dearest!*" She leaped to her feet, furious. How dare Madame talk as if she and Rosamund were her dearest friends? When she had done nothing but work behind their backs since her return, had cut them off from Papa King, had even – Emily was more than ever certain of this – been responsible for all the nightmarish happenings since the night of the birthday party? Now, here she was, trying to use Emily and Rosamund's predicament to attract the attention back to herself. It was almost more than Emily could bear.

At that moment, thankfully, Madame disappeared from the screen. Her face was replaced by images of weeping fans, the vigil outside Miniver House, and finally, an interviewer called Serena Simpson whom Emily knew well from her own TV appearances.

"So, tell me, Superintendent," said Serena. "With all the rumours about the Miniver sisters being murdered, should fans be bracing themselves for the worst?"

The picture cut to a serious-looking policeman. "At this point in time, we have no way of knowing for certain," he said, in an official voice. "However, we hold grave fears for their safety. They are small and vulnerable persons. The entire force is on heightened alert until we find them."

"What about the suspect you have in custody? Is it true that the person you have arrested is the Minivers' own housekeeper?"

"The person is no longer in police custody. I'm afraid I can't comment."

"What about the rumours of a plot? Some people are talking of a huge conspiracy—"

"No. Let me get this straight, there is *no* conspiracy," said the superintendent, and Emily thought he sounded almost angry. "There is no point in fans engaging in idle speculation. As soon as there is news we will let people know. In the meantime, we encourage Minivers fans not to panic, but to keep their eyes and ears open. Any suspected sightings should be reported by telephoning the new Minivers Crisis Line or your local police station. We promise every call will be taken seriously."

"Thank you, Superintendent. And you can find that free-phone number now, on the bottom of your screen. Back to the palace, and—"

Emily switched off the set before Madame could reappear. It was too late though: her fragile peace had been wrecked. She sat down on the table and looked once more out of the tinted porthole. It was hard to see much, but there seemed to be more boats moving about on the river. People were shouting and a man was calling through a megaphone. Then the police launch roared past again, so fast that *Bella-Mae* rocked wildly at her moorings. Emily had to clutch the table or be tipped off.

It was no use pretending. Every moment she spent on the boat she was in danger of discovery, and unless she chanced to be found by a sympathetic fan whom she could persuade to help her, she would be caught and never seen or heard of again. Yet even this dismal thought brought hope. For there were sympathetic fans – a lot of them. Emily had just seen them on the television, and though they were mostly strangers, there were some fans she knew very well. Out of all these, the one she was fondest of was Lindsey Smith, the Life President of the Minivers Fan Club. If Emily could contact Lindsey, she would be sure to help her, no matter what.

This decision helped Emily feel much better. There was however, a problem. Lindsey had been sick and was staying with an aunt outside the city. In case she had trouble finding her, Emily made a mental shortlist of temporary hiding places. Some were so clever she felt certain she would never be found; nevertheless, the rest of the day passed much less pleasantly. The closed-up boat grew hotter and stuffier. Emily mopped her face with a damp cloth and drank glass after glass of warm, stale water, but the heat was nothing compared to the boredom. The people who owned *Bella-Mae* were obviously more interested in boating than reading. Their magazines had titles like *Helmsman* and *Seafarer* and their books were all full of crossword puzzles that had already been done. Emily did her best with the magazines, but they made dreary reading and she could not help fretting about Rosamund and Millamant.

At last the sun went down over the water in a rush of orange and scarlet. Emily turned on the lights and made herself a dinner of tinned ham and pineapple. It took her absolutely ages to get the tins open, and the ham turned out to be salty and not very nice. To make matters worse, when Emily went to get another drink, nothing but a trickle came out of the tap. Over the course of the day, she had pumped the water tank dry.

Now there was nothing else for it: she had to leave. Emily packed her clothes and a few provisions into a plastic bag and climbed on to the bunk so she could look through the open hatch on to the deck. Just as she remembered, a rubber dinghy was lying upside down on *Bella-Mae*'s roof. Emily squirmed out on to the deck and started picking at the ropes that secured it. They were hard work for her tiny fingers, and as she crouched in the darkness trying to free them, her ears were drawn by an unexpected noise.

It was the sound of a boat being stealthily rowed towards her. Emily hardly noticed it at first, for the river was a very noisy place, with motorboats and ferries and the sound of traffic from the nearby motorway. But at night even soft voices carry over water, and as the approaching boat came very close, she became aware of two men quietly talking between oar strokes.

"It's very unusual for the Fredericks to be at the boat during the week," said a voice Emily did not know. "They only ever take *Bella-Mae* out on the weekends."

"When did you first notice someone was there?" said a second, familiar voice. Instantly, Emily huddled down against the dinghy's rubber hull. It was Titus.

"I think there's been someone on board all day," said the first man. "The TV's been on, and there's been water coming out of the outlet on the port side. The funny thing is, the boat's been completely shut up. No one in sight at all. And then, when I realized the Fredericks' car wasn't at the jetty. . ."

"That was very observant of you, Mr Warner," said Titus. "Of course, we must follow up every lead. Now if we can just tie up here, next to the stern. Quietly, we don't want to disturb anyone down in the cabin. . ."

There was a soft clunk as the small hull hit the big one. *Bella-Mae* rocked gently at her moorings. The men were talking in whispers now, and Emily could not hear what they were saying. She felt the yacht shudder slightly as the men climbed on to *Bella-Mae*'s duckboard, and then on to her deck. The door to the cabin creaked open. There was a moment's silence and Emily heard them moving about inside.

Emily stood up quickly. She had only moments before the two men came back out on deck. Stooping as low as she could, Emily ran like a cat along the port side towards the stern. She heard voices in the cabin – "She's here!" and then, "She's *been* here," corrected Titus – and wished, since she had been silly enough to turn the light on, that she could at least have slowed them down by turning it off before she had gone out on deck.

Emily scrambled over the stern and dropped down on to the yacht's duckboard. She had assumed she would have to swim for it, as fast and quietly as she was able. But now, for the first time since her escape had begun, she had the most enormous bit of luck. Titus's dinghy was tied up to *Bella-Mae*'s stern. And the knot that secured it was so loose that even Emily would be able to undo it.

Emily scrambled into the dinghy. She loosed it from its mooring and immediately, it started drifting downstream. Emily reached for the oars, which were shipped, and hopelessly long and heavy for her. She managed to lift the blade of one over the side, and tugged and shoved it against the water with all her puny strength. The dinghy turned aimlessly around and continued to drift.

"Hey, there!"

Emily looked up. An unknown man, presumably Mr Warner, had come out of *Bella-Mae's* cabin and was waving at her from the stern. Emily gave a cry of fear. She grabbed the second oar, but it was impossible to manoeuvre with just one hand, and it slipped and fell into the river with a loud splash. Titus jumped up on to the side of the boat and called her name.

"Emily?"

"Go away!" shouted Emily. "Go away!"

"We have Rosamund, Emily. We have her now. You know what that means. You can't get away. Help your sister: she needs you. Come back to the yacht and stop this."

For half a second, Emily faltered. The thought of Rosamund in Titus's power was so terrifying she literally did not know what to do. Titus was crouching on the side of the boat, and a pleading tone entered his voice.

Emily could see his pale face with its blue eyes and fair lank hair, and the expression she had always thought of as so kind and friendly. Then she saw the strip of white sticking plaster on his forehead, and remembered how he had tricked her in the car park. With all her strength, Emily picked up the other oar and stood up in the middle of the dinghy.

"*Liar!*" she shouted. "You haven't got Rosamund. And you won't get me, either!" She lifted the oar as menacingly as she could, which was only a few inches, and overbalanced with a thump in the bottom of the boat. The dinghy see-sawed back and forth, and she heard Titus shout again from *Bella-Mae*.

"This is your last chance, Emily. You can't go anywhere. Do you think I can't see you aren't even strong enough to pick up that oar?"

"Come any closer, and I'll thump you with it!" As she spoke, Emily's eyes fell on something she had not seen earlier: a tiny outboard motor, bolted to the dinghy's stern. Titus had obviously avoided using it because he had wanted to approach *Bella-Mae* as quietly as possible.

Emily grabbed the outboard and swung it into the water. She had no idea how it worked, but there was a starter cord on it, a little like a lawnmower. She yanked the cord as hard as she could, falling over a second time amidships. The motor coughed unpromisingly, and behind her, there was a loud splash in the water. Titus had dived off *Bella-Mae* and was swimming towards her.

"Help!" Emily screamed. "*Help me!*"

Other boats were cruising up and down the river, but not one of them seemed to realize she was there. Again Emily yanked the starter cord, and again the motor did not start. Her fingers fumbled with the controls, flicking chokes, switches, *anything*, if it would only make the wretched motor start. The splashing in the water grew louder. Titus was only half a dozen strokes away. Emily closed her eyes. With all her might, she yanked back on the starter cord one last time.

The motor gave a sputtering roar and burst into life. Emily shrieked with joy. She grabbed the tiller and twisted the throttle. The dinghy spun out of control in crazy circles across the water. Emily twisted the throttle almost to maximum. The dinghy spun faster and faster; she heard Titus shout in terror, and saw him hastily ducking under as she skated narrowly by in a shower of stinking diesel fumes and river water.

"Mess with a Miniver," Emily shouted, "and you'll be sorry!" She spun the dinghy between two moored yachts into the open river, straightened up, and raced triumphantly away.

9

THE BRIDGE HOUSE

Millamant was cold.

It was almost summer, and the room she was shut up in was airless, hot and stuffy. But Millamant was not just a prisoner. Ever since her arrival, she had been desperately ill. Her head ached, her joints throbbed, and her throat was so sore she could hardly swallow. Her mouth was dry from lack of water, and she had not eaten since her arrest on Monday morning. The very walls seemed to thud and vibrate. Millamant lay on the floor, in the darkness and the dust, and shivered from head to foot with sickness and terror.

She felt as she had done when she was at school, an unattractive, tiny girl almost as round as she was high. The other children had bullied her. They called her "runt" and made her life a misery, stealing Millamant's books and lunches, imprisoning her in lockers, forcibly dressing her in ridiculous clothes made for dolls or babies. Wherever she went, people stared and pointed at her. Millamant had known she was a freak. In those days, nobody had wanted her, not even her own parents. She had been unhappy, frightened, and alone.

When Millamant had grown up, things had not been very much better. She had still been bullied, though grown-ups were cleverer at it than children; and though she was a much tougher person because of the way she had been treated, she had still been miserably alone. Then, through a series of accidents and some small bravery on her part, Emily and Rosamund Miniver had come into her life. Like Millamant, they were small, but unlike Millamant, people loved them for it. When baby Rosamund was first put in her arms, Millamant had known at last why she had been born the size she was. She had determined, then and there, that neither Emily nor Rosamund would ever suffer for being small, that no one would ever call them freaks, or hurt or taunt them. Millamant loved Rosamund and Emily more than she loved herself. Now, sick and imprisoned as she was, she could think of nothing else but where they were, whether they were safe, and worst of all, whether they were even still alive.

Hot, salty tears flowed down Millamant's cheeks. *I should have known,* she thought despairingly. *I knew what Madame was like, better than any of them. It was stupid to hope she might have changed.*

But you had no proof, Millamant, her own commonsense argued back. *There was no one you could have spoken to, and anyway, you can't accuse somebody, just because of something they did when they were a teenager. And you did write to Gibraltar.*

I still should have done more, said her tearful half. And indeed, Millamant had been afraid for a long time that something terrible might happen. She had seen it start after Papa King's stroke, when the newspapers had begun to print pictures of the Minivers that were not quite perfect, and stories that were not quite kind. Millamant had known, as Rosamund and Emily could not, that love, especially the love of people who do not really know you, is a fragile thing. She had known too, that though Rosamund and Emily worked hard for the love their fans gave them, they had never completely earned it. It was Papa King who had ordained that the Minivers should be everybody's darlings. He had set Emily and Rosamund up for the people of Artemisia to worship, to take their minds off complaining about the way he ruled. He had known that, because they loved the Minivers, the people would also love him. Papa King had been very clever, Millamant thought. And, of course, the cleverest thing about what he had done was that, from the moment of Rosamund's arrival, Papa King had loved the Minivers himself. They had filled a hole in his own life that was deeper than he would have admitted, a hole made by disappointment and Madame's betrayal.

Millamant had a fair idea of just how much Papa King had looked after Rosamund and Emily, and how many bad things he had stopped from happening to them. But now that he was ill, his love was no protection. Rosamund and Emily were completely on their own. In the face of Madame's hatred, there was no clear escape for any of them.

The conference room at Miniver House was the only room with doors and ceilings of ordinary height. It had been designed for the Miniver sisters to hold parties for normal-sized visitors, and they also used it for their press conferences. Since the events of Black Monday, it had been cleared out and used for other purposes. The conference room, with its lofty ceilings and blue plush carpet, was now the site of Operation Miniver, and the call centre for the Minivers Crisis Line.

Around the room, men and women wearing headsets were furiously logging incoming calls. Others watched tape after tape of closed-circuit TV footage. Blue-shirted security officers and police detectives came and went, and on a wall at the far end of the room, a huge map of Artemisia was dotted with coloured flags, marking all reported sightings of the Minivers.

Titus was standing in front of the map, twiddling a blue flag between his fingers. The blue flags stood for Emily, the red ones for Rosamund, and the yellow ones, which were by far the greatest number, stood for unconfirmed reports by members of the public. Titus's eyes were fixed on a blue flag in the middle of the river. He stared at the map for a moment longer. Then he leaned forward, and carefully pushed the flag he was holding into the cork.

"Can you give me a moment?" said Ron. Titus nodded and the two men withdrew to a corner. Ron sat down at a desk covered with papers and handed Titus a typed report. "I've just debriefed the team that handled Emily's call," Ron said. "You were right. It was logged at four o'clock this morning, to Lindsey Smith at her aunt's house in Somerford. Luckily, after your tip-off, we'd already taken Lindsey into custody, but the aunt didn't play the game as well as we'd hoped. The plan was to keep Emily talking as long as possible while we traced the call, but she was smart enough to realize something was up. By the time my team reached the phone box, Emily had gone."

"Hmm," said Titus. He chewed his thumbnail. "Still,

we've come very close on at least two occasions. Have you tried the places I suggested?"

Ron nodded. "Offices, record companies, dressmakers, hairdressers – every building and every person we can think of that they know." He shook his head. "We're running out of time. Every day increases the chance that somebody will find out the truth, and when that happens we'll be so deep in trouble it'll take a lifetime to dig ourselves out. Including you."

"I know that," said Titus calmly. "I told Madame to wait, but she wouldn't listen." He stood up. "Widen the search," he ordered. "Emily's obviously trying to contact fans. I'll send you a list of our club's committee members for the last five years, and any other prominent fans I can think of. After that, try the city hotels and big shops. Hotels like the Artemisia where they've been to functions, department stores like Eastman's and Delaney's where they've shopped."

Ron stared at him. "That's impossible!" he exploded. "You're talking about days of work. I've got a family, you know. Young Alex's problems are getting worse – my wife's worn to a thread. Besides, I've already spent most of the Minivers' security budget. If Madame wants this sort of effort, the palace treasury is going to have to cough up."

"You can forget about that," said Titus. "Madame will

never spend her own money when she can spend somebody else's. All the same, I honestly don't think it's going to take that much longer. We just have to think more like Minivers. We have to imagine how they're feeling and what they'd do."

"Just at the moment," said Ron, "I'd rather not do that."

Titus smiled. "That, my friend, is the difference between us."

Eastman's, on George Street, was the oldest and poshest department store in Artemisia. It was the place where the wealthiest and most important citizens went to shop, and more often than not, one of the places its distinctive green and white delivery vans called into was Miniver House. Rosamund and Emily Miniver were regular customers at Eastman's. They shopped there for things like gifts, which had to be normal-sized, and the exceedingly polite staff were happy to open the building after hours so they could shop in private.

Since Black Monday, Eastman's display windows had been draped with black silk curtains. In the centre of each window hung a floodlit portrait of either Emily, looking sweet and thoughtful, or Rosamund, at her poised and elegant best. The windows had attracted a great deal of attention, which was what their designer had intended, and ever since the Minivers' disappearance, Eastman's had been doing a brisk trade in merchandise. The "Rosamund" range of cosmetics had done particularly well, along with the lavender-based "Emily" and rose-based "Rosamund" perfumes. In the toy department, so many Miniver playhouses had been sold that it would be at least three months before the store filled all the orders.

It was in the toy department, shortly after midnight, that a tiny figure emerged like a shadow from the storeroom. It had been hovering for some time, carefully monitoring what was happening in the store. When the big glass doors were closed on George Street, Eastman's came alive with cleaners and people putting new stock on the shelves, and for several hours it was almost as busy as it was during the day.

By midnight, most of this work had been done, and the intruder felt safe enough to venture from her hiding place. She ran the length of the toy department, keeping as close as she could to the shelves. At the end, she crouched low by a stack of Minivers jigsaw puzzles and waited for a nearby security camera to sweep past. As soon as the camera pointed away, the intruder dropped on to her stomach. She slid like a baby octopus under the shelves and out into Children's Wear. Here she stopped by the very smallest clothes, and pulled a pink T-shirt off a shelf. The tiny thief added a pair of shorts, some underpants and matching socks to her swag, and quickly shoved it all into a small purple backpack.

The thief moved silently from department to department. She took a knife from Kitchenware, a small torch from Camping, and a Compact Artemisia Street Directory from Books. In Electrical, she found a miniature radio and spare batteries. Finally, she did a commando crawl through Shoes and arrived at her final destination, Gourmet Gifts.

Gourmet Gifts was adjacent to the store cafè, which was locked up for the night. For a moment, the intruder looked mournfully through the glass at the cake cabinets and refrigerators full of leftover fresh food. But they were impossible to get into, so she turned instead to the shelves of expensive chocolates and prettily packaged pots of jam. As she put the last box of biscuits into her bag, the intruder glanced at her watch. It was twenty-four minutes past midnight. She had seven minutes exactly before the security guard came back on his round.

Quickly and carefully, watching always for security cameras and keeping to the shadows, the intruder crept back to the storeroom. By the time the security guard arrived, Emily Miniver had disappeared. She had vanished amongst the disused SALE signs and out of season Easter Bunnies, as if she had never been there at all.

Shortly after dawn on Thursday morning, a white car pulled up at a curious bridge on the outskirts of Artemisia. The bridge had a stone archway at either end under which the traffic drove, and each archway was in turn topped by a square turret with windows. People had once lived in them, for the Bridge House had been built as a home for the tollkeeper, in the days when people were expected to pay to go over the bridge. Now it was largely forgotten, except by people who found it useful to have a place to hide things.

The white car turned off the main road and drove down a private driveway. It went through a gate at the bottom and parked beside a wooden door, set into the stone. The driver's door opened and Madame got out. She was not in a good mood. It was several days since she had slept properly, and she was still fuming over Papa King's unexpected birthday present to Rosamund Miniver. The fact that he had made her deliver it was even worse. It was, Madame thought, just the sort of sly and sneaky thing she would have expected him to do.

Madame slammed her car door shut and stomped up some steps to the Bridge House door. She did not like this part of what she was doing, not because she felt sorry for Millamant, whom she detested, but because, like all bullies, she was at heart a coward. Madame knew she was skating on very thin ice. She had been telling a lot of lies lately, and while her conscience was not particularly bothered by this, the thought of what might happen if one of the Minivers unexpectedly reappeared bothered her a lot.

Madame knocked on the door. A moment later, it was opened by Ron. He was unshaven, and looked very grumpy.

Madame pushed into the cramped stone hallway. "Has she said anything?"

"No. I've been asking the same questions over and over, and she hasn't said a word." Ron followed Madame up the wooden stairs to the turret. "She really is very sick. I don't know whether she's refusing to say anything, or whether she's just too ill to speak."

"Millamant? Too ill to speak? I don't think so."

They reached the door of the turret room. Ron unlocked it and Madame stepped through the low doorway into Millamant's prison. At first she could see nothing, for the light was turned off to avoid attracting attention from outside. Then her eyes became accustomed to the dimness, and she saw that she stood in a squalid little room, with two very high paned windows. A glow of orange street lamps filtered in, and there was a low rumble of traffic going over the bridge beneath. Madame, who was accustomed to dirt and neglect, was unmoved by the dust and broken furniture and the sheer nastiness of the unemptied slop bucket. But the room was hot and almost airless, and she could not stop the film of sweat that broke out on her forehead and the back of her neck.

A small grey shape lay slumped in the corner of the room. It looked like a bundle of old clothes, wrapped in a blanket and thrown on to the scrap-heap. Only the rasp of its breathing told Madame it was alive. Madame went up to it, and stood for a moment looking down.

"Millamant."

The bundle stirred and moaned, but it did not, or would not, sit up. Madame waited a moment. When there was no further response from the prisoner she stooped, and delicately took hold of one of her stubby fair-haired plaits. Bit by bit, the blanket fell off, and Millamant sat up. She had no choice, for Madame was pulling on her hair. Though her face was as grey as the blanket, Millamant did not utter so much as a whimper.

111

"Millamant, I need to know where Rosamund put the key." Madame was not much of a talker, and she did not see any point in beating about the bush. "Ron's people have searched Miniver House from top to bottom, and they haven't been able to find it. I know it wasn't on her when she was kidnapped. Where is it?"

"I don't know." Millamant's voice was a dry whisper. "I can't tell you."

"You're very thirsty, aren't you, Millamant? I know Rosamund and Emily well; they never keep secrets from you. Tell me where the key is, and you can have a glass of water."

"Go jump, Karen." Millamant coughed. "You can't make me tell you something I don't know. If Rosamund hid the key, then the only person who knows where it is, is her."

"Suppose I ask her, then?" said Madame spitefully. "Rosamund's my prisoner too, you know. I'm sure you wouldn't want her to suffer, when she's so small and delicate."

For the first time, a look of fear came into Millamant's eyes. She stared hard at Madame, and looked across at Ron. Her face relaxed and she shook her head. "You're lying," she said. "You don't have Rosamund. If she was really your prisoner, you wouldn't be asking me these questions. Rosamund doesn't even know why the key's important. If you'd asked her, she'd have told you quickly enough where you could find it."

"Rosamund is dead," said Madame. "She died, trying to escape my people; she fell under a train. It was in all the papers this morning."

"Oh, come on, Karen." A tinge of contempt crept into Millamant's voice. "You can do better than that. Rosamund would no more fall under a train than you would tell the truth. Do you think I don't know what you're like? I remember you before Papa King sent you away. Ill-natured, bad-tempered, proud. You haven't changed a bit, for all the years you were gone. You were a bully from the day you were born."

"Maybe I still am." Madame's pale cheeks turned an angry red. "I might not have killed Rosamund yet, but we're looking for her and Emily, too. The whole of Artemisia is reporting to me, now. I will find the Minivers, and when I do I'll make sure you're the first to know what I do to them." She gave Millamant a shove that sent her thudding against the wall. "No food for the prisoner again today, Ron. Give her enough water to keep her alive, but no more. Keep on questioning her and don't let up. I'll be back again tomorrow morning, at eight o'clock."

10

LIVIA

It was Friday morning, and Livia Wallace lay on her front verandah watching the dawn.

She was surrounded by lattice, soft light and birdsong. From her hammock she could see the yellow glow on the wall of her house growing slowly richer and deeper. The faint scent of frangipani filled the morning air, and the exposed tin of the verandah roof above her head began to creak gently as the sun warmed it.

Livia untangled herself from her blanket and swung out of her hammock. The front door was unlocked, for her house was so hidden by trees and morning glory vines behind its picket fence that she was not afraid of strangers coming in uninvited. Livia had inherited the house from her grandfather, the City Archivist. When she had moved in, it had been sad and grey, but now, as she pushed open the door and went into the living room, it dripped with colour like a giant lollipop at a funfair.

The walls were yellow and pink, like sunshine and

flowers. The curtains were covered with splashes of daisies and the ceiling was painted blue with white wispy clouds around the dangling light-fitting. Above the small oak bookcases filled with children's books and diaries were paintings of gigantic roses. Livia had painted them herself, and she had embroidered the cushions that dotted the deep pink sofa. Livia hurried through the room on bare feet, and went down the back steps on to the thick coarse grass of her back lawn.

The sun was just showing over the screen of trees. Livia stood looking at the riot of orange nasturtiums, and the fat round pumpkins in her vegetable bed. Then her eyes fell on the clothes line. A blue dustcoat hung there, cold and damp with dew. Livia's early morning happiness evaporated. In a little over an hour, she would have to put the dustcoat on, go into the archives, and leave everything beautiful she had created here behind.

Livia hated working at the archives. She was sure there must be something better she could do, like paint pictures, or write stories, or sew clothes to sell in the markets. But her mother had worked in the archives, and her grandfather had been City Archivist, so it had been difficult for her to say no to the job. The archive jobs were very well paid, and people who did not care about the darkness and the dust fought hard to get them. Livia did care. She craved sunshine and brightness, and she hated being shut up, which was why she slept outside every night. In fact, if it had not been for her cousin Karen needing her help, Livia was sure she would have given up long ago.

Poor Karen. Livia did not know her cousin well, but she could not believe she deserved to be so badly treated. As a little girl, Livia had thought it very exciting to have relatives who lived in the palace with Papa King. Then something had gone wrong, and Cousin Karen and her mother, Aunt Susan, had disappeared. Nobody had ever explained why, but Livia remembered how upset her grandfather had been, so upset, in fact, that he would never let anybody talk about it. It was Cousin Karen who had told Livia how Papa King had rejected her for Rosamund Miniver, and how the true story of what had happened was hidden in the Most Secret Room in the archives. Sometimes, Livia did not quite like the way her cousin talked about the Most Secret Room. She hated the way Karen kept hassling her about it, and it would have been easier to feel enthusiastic if her cousin had been a nicer person. On the other hand, she could not blame Cousin Karen for feeling hard done by. Livia only wished she could find what she was looking for, so that she could give up her job at the archives and never go back.

Reluctantly, Livia unpegged her dustcoat from the

line, and went inside. She buttered some bread, put an egg on to boil, and made herself a pot of tea. On the kitchen table was her diary. Livia took it everywhere, and it was open at a drawing she had made at work the day before. The picture showed a man with a dark beard and long hair in a ponytail, a porter who had just started working at the archives. It was a good likeness, but there was something about the man's expression that made Livia uncomfortable. He had, she thought, a face that was full of secrets, and not all of them were his own.

The egg timer beeped. Livia propped the diary up against the teapot and cut her bread into dippers. While she ate her breakfast, she read through the entries for the last few days.

Monday, 11th October
Late for work because of a traffic jam. Measured the walls in rooms 8-4 and 8-5. They match the building plan exactly, so the Most Secret Room is not there.

Saw that new porter, Gibraltar, on the lower levels again. I think he's watching me.

Tuesday, 12th October
Two phone calls from Cousin Karen. Still no luck with the Most Secret Room.

Wednesday, 13th October
Gibraltar in very early this morning with a big backpack.
Spotted him searching cupboards on level seven.

Something about Gibraltar makes me
uncomfortable. He's always somewhere he shouldn't be.
I'm going to watch him carefully.

Thursday, 14th October
Cousin Karen keeps phoning. She's very cross that I'm
not getting anywhere.

Followed Gibraltar down to level seven. I stopped
him outside one of the big cupboards nobody uses. He
said he was getting something for the Deputy Archivist,
but I know he was lying.

After he had gone, I saw something moving behind
the stacks. It was too quick for me, but it was far too
big to be a rat.

Livia pushed aside her empty plate and picked up a pencil. She sucked the end thoughtfully, then turned to the next page of the diary and wrote,

Friday 15th October
Maybe Gibraltar is an enemy of Cousin Karen. One
way or another, I'm going to find out what he's up to.

Livia underlined the words with a determined flourish. Then she dropped her diary into her bag and her plate into the sink and, picking up her dustcoat, headed off to work.

"I hate this bag," said Rosamund, in a muffled voice. "I still don't see why you couldn't leave me in the caravan."

"Because it's not safe," said Gibraltar. "They're widening their search and I don't want to leave you on your own."

His booted feet rang out on the metal staircase as he descended into the archive basements. For the last few days, Gibraltar had been going to work early, so Rosamund could be hidden safely before he started. So far, they had been lucky, but it was still dangerous. A sharp-eyed person would have noticed that the top flap on the canvas backpack slung over his shoulder hung much more heavily than it should have for its size, and from time to time it moved, as the tiny person inside shifted about and tried to see out.

Luckily, this morning they were almost alone in the building. On the fifth level down, Gibraltar turned into a dingily lit corridor. Its walls were lined with metal shelves, full of dusty cardboard boxes. The boxes were so old that several had fallen apart and dropped their contents on to the floor. Gibraltar walked past them, turned into a slip of a room and shut the door. He took a key out of his dustcoat pocket, locked them in, and slung the backpack on to the ground.

"You can come out now."

Rosamund pushed back the flap and emerged. If her fans could have seen her, they would have been shocked. Her glossy hair was dull from lack of washing and tied in a simple plait; her face was pale, and she was wearing an oversized T-shirt that made her look like a doll-sized scarecrow. The shirt was black to blend in with the shadows where she had to hide. Gibraltar had left Rosamund in a different hiding place every day: in cupboards, storerooms, and even, briefly, in a filing cabinet. This room had nothing in it but empty cardboard boxes, long since forgotten by whoever it was who had dumped them.

Gibraltar shrugged several times and rubbed his aching neck. "You know, you're much heavier than you look," he said. "I think you must be starting to put on weight."

"I'm not a gram over fifteen kilos," retorted Rosamund. "My doctor tells me that's exactly the right weight for my height. If there's any Miniver who's going to get fat, it's Emily. She eats far more chocolate than is good for her." Her lip trembled at the mention of her sister's name, and suddenly, as she had many times in the last few days, she started to cry.

120

Gibraltar crouched down so that he was at her level. He had guessed from the beginning that Rosamund had never been a particularly brave person. She had never needed to be, for she had always had other people to shield her from harm. Now those other people were gone or had betrayed her, and she had only a complete stranger to help her. Gibraltar did not blame her for wanting to burst into tears, but he did not encourage her either. At first, Rosamund had cried all the time, until she made herself sick. As the days went by, Gibraltar had noticed that her crying fits had become shorter, and that she had got better and better at controlling them. This time, after three or four minutes, Rosamund gulped, stopped, and blew her nose loudly on the hem of her T-shirt.

"I just wish I knew what to do," she said. "Emily's so little, and I can't help thinking it's all my fault. I'm so afraid she's dead."

"If she is," said Gibraltar, "then you must learn to live alone. But I think she is probably alive."

"I hope so," said Rosamund. "I think so, too, most of the time. If she were dead, I think I would know." She banged her hand against her chest. "Here. I would feel it. But then, I keep hearing in the news how they're searching for her body and I can't help wondering. I can't be sure. That's what's so hard about this. All of it would be so much easier if we were just together."

"You shouldn't believe what you hear on the radio and read in the papers," said Gibraltar sternly. "You of all people should know they're full of lies. How many bad, or embarrassing stories did Papa King stop the papers from printing about you and your sister? Now someone else is controlling what they say, only the lies they tell are ones you do not want to hear. Do you really believe Millamant murdered your sister?"

"Of course not!" said Rosamund. "Millamant would never hurt us. But suppose somebody else did? Suppose Madame has murdered Emily? That's what I'm really afraid of."

"If Madame had murdered Emily, she would not be searching for her so frantically," said Gibraltar. "That is the truth behind the news stories, and you have to hold on to it." He put his hand into his backpack and handed Rosamund a torch. "Take this. Stay in here and keep the door locked. I'll be back as soon as I can get away, at morning tea."

From the shadow of a concrete pillar, Livia watched Gibraltar come out of the room and walk away. She had seen him go in carrying his backpack and come out without it. Livia knew better than anyone that the archives were full of forgotten rooms and that Gibraltar had no reason to be leaving his things there.

Livia went to the door and gently touched the handle with her left hand. It was locked, but this time she had come prepared. Livia brought her right hand out from under her dustcoat. She put the jemmy she had been using in her searches for the Most Secret Room into the door jamb and leaned on it, sharply, with all her weight.

There was a crack of splintering wood and the door swung open. Livia could have sworn she saw a torch flick off inside. She felt anxiously for a light switch. There was one there, but the bulb must have been broken, for it snapped uselessly back and forth, and the room remained in darkness.

Livia took a torch out of her pocket. For a moment she waited in the doorway, jemmy in one hand, torch in the other, listening intently. She could almost hear her own heartbeat. Another moment passed, and she heard a tiny rustle and the sound of someone breathing, quick and light.

Livia's courage almost failed her. Her hand sweated on the jemmy and it took all her will power to turn on her torch and shine it into the room.

Gibraltar's backpack sat in the middle of the floor. It was empty, though Livia knew it had been carried in full. There was nothing else in the room except piles of mouldering cardboard boxes, jumbled together in heaps against the walls. Livia swept her torch from corner to corner.

"I know you're in here." Her voice sounded high and wobbly. "You might as well come out. I can hear you breathing."

There was no reply. The thin sound of breathing stopped, as if the fugitive had held their breath. Livia waited, silently counting while she shone her torchlight over the boxes. When she reached twenty, she stopped.

"All right then. If you won't come out, I'll have to find you and force you out."

Screwing up her courage, Livia advanced on the boxes. She kicked the first one out of the way, then started hooking them from the pile with the jemmy. As they flew into the corridor, she heard a gasp. There was a scrabbling sound, as the person who was hiding worked their way further back into the heap. Livia realized that whoever it was felt as frightened as she did. It gave her courage and she picked up speed.

At that instant, with a tremendous shriek, something small and dark shot out of the pile of boxes. Livia dropped her jemmy with a clang. She grabbed at the shape as it went past, fell over with a thud, then jumped up and ran after it into the corridor.

"Stop!" she cried. "*Stop!*"

11

THE CARDBOARD BOX

"Gibraltar! Gibraltar!" shouted Rosamund. She picked up her T-shirt and raced away on bare feet down the corridor. "Where are you? *Help me!*"

Running footsteps sounded behind her. A woman's voice shouted for her to stop. Rosamund glanced back over her shoulder. The woman in the blue dustcoat had emerged from the room with the cardboard boxes, and was in rapid and determined pursuit. Rosamund dodged around a corner into another corridor. At the end was a swing door and staircases leading to the other levels. With more instinct than thought, Rosamund burst through the door and jumped on to the metal handrail, like a cowboy into the saddle.

Down she slid, gathering speed, slipping further and further away from Gibraltar, help, and safety. She did not stop on the sixth level, but jumped straight on to the next rail and continued her downward slide. The woman in the dustcoat appeared on the landing two floors above. She shouted something Rosamund could not understand and started hurrying down two, three steps at a time until she stumbled and nearly pitched headlong. *Ha!* thought Rosamund. Her courage revived and she jumped off the second railing on to a landing labelled 7. Some inner warning system told her it would be best not to go further down, so she shoved open another door and ran through into a basement worse than any she had passed through yet.

It smelled. The fifth level had been dim and dusty, but the seventh was dank, as if the damp from the river was seeping through its concrete walls. Rosamund, who was fast becoming breathless from so much running, turned into a side corridor and slowed to a walk. A stitch was starting up in her side and she realized she must find somewhere to hide before she was discovered and caught.

There was a door ahead, hanging on broken hinges. Rosamund squeezed around the jamb into a room so dark she could barely see. Almost immediately she crashed into something and yelped a word of which Millamant would certainly not have approved. Fortunately, her eyes were already adjusting to the poor light. After a moment Rosamund was able to see that she had walked into a huge chunk of cement, which had fallen out of the crumbling ceiling on to the floor.

She was in what seemed to be a storeroom for everything that was broken and unwanted. Drawerless filing cabinets jumbled with mountains of office chairs and rusted metal shelves. Some shelves contained boxes and papers, but they were mostly empty and festooned with dirt. Rosamund limped a few paces through what felt like a mass of slightly wet, fallen leaves. It was several moments before she realized she was actually walking through a litter of chewed and shredded paper, spotted with tiny dark marks that she recognized to her horror as droppings.

"*Ugh!*" Rosamund recoiled. She banged into a teetering set of shelves and a heavy box of papers, glued together from the damp, fell with an explosive thud at her feet. The shelves rocked dangerously and began to topple; Rosamund wrapped her arms around her head and screamed. There was no time to get out of the way. With an enormous crash, the shelves fell forward and slammed into the set in front of them.

If Rosamund had been only a few inches taller, the shelves would have crushed her skull. Instead, they showered her with years of dirt and accumulated mouse droppings and left her standing, blinded and cringing, in a stinking cloud of dust. Rosamund cried out, swallowed an involuntary lungful, and began coughing as she had never coughed before. She was still choking for breath, trying helplessly to stop, when the broken door grated open. A torch shone painfully in her streaming eyes. Rosamund blinked up at the woman in the dustcoat. The fight went out of her and she surrendered without another word.

The cardboard box sat on the Toy Department floor. It was not particularly big, though it was the largest of several awaiting collection that morning. It might have held a doll's house, a giant teddy bear, or a jumbo-sized box of building blocks. An Eastman's delivery docket had been stuck on the top, and was addressed in a small but firm black hand to:

THE MINIVERS FAN CLUB (HQ)
46 BERRY STREET
ARTEMISIA EAST
ATTENTION: WAREHOUSE

On the box itself was written in the same small hand URGENT DELIVERY – FRIDAY.

Not far away in Children's Wear, two uniformed women were going over a rack of T-shirts. They were too busy to notice the pile of boxes, let alone the unusual address label on the biggest carton. One woman had a big chain of keys hanging from her belt. The other was dressed in a blue skirt and jacket, with a red M monogrammed on the pocket. She wore a plastic apron and gloves, and was carefully brushing sooty black powder over the rail and several coathangers. It was Primrose, from the Miniver House security team.

"Well, I think that's pretty definite." Primrose straightened up and dusted the fingerprint powder from her hands. "I'll have to get a match for the prints. We've already confirmed the set in your Book Department and when you check the rest of the security tapes. . ."

"I've got two staff working on them right now," said the other woman, who was Eastman's Security Manager. "I'm sorry we've been so slow to pick up on this. After-hours intruders normally get caught quite quickly here. She shouldn't have been able to leave the building."

"No matter. The Miniver won't get very far on those little legs," said Primrose. She thought of the bonus that awaited whoever tracked down Emily and Rosamund: a whole year's salary payable as a lump sum, without tax. All the members of the Minivers Security Force were desperate to earn it, though not all of them knew what would happen to the Miniver sisters when they were found. Primrose did know. But then, she did not like Rosamund and Emily Miniver, and did not particularly care what became of them.

A workman came into the department and started loading the cardboard boxes on to a trolley. Primrose thought of what she would do with the money when she got it. She was still deciding which tropical island to visit when the workman put the last and biggest box on to his trolley and wheeled it away.

The trolley trundled out of the door, along a lino-floored passage and into a service lift. In the basement loading dock, the first of the morning's deliveries was about to go out. A man was sitting on the tailgate of a truck, reading a newspaper. On the front page was a photograph of the Minivers and the headline *STILL MISSING*.

"Load 'er up, Jason," he said, folding the paper.

The man with the trolley began tossing the boxes across to him. The truck driver caught them deftly and slid them one by one into the back of the truck.

"Careful!" He pointed to a red FRAGILE sticker on the side of the largest carton. Jason handed the last box over carefully. The driver stowed it inside and folded up the tailgate. He climbed into the cab and started the engine, and the truck rolled out into the morning traffic and drove away.

Livia ran down the front steps of the archives, her dustcoat flapping wildly. Her stockings were torn, she was covered in dust, and if anybody had seen the expression on her face, they must have thought she had just seen something terrifying.

Livia dragged her car keys out of her handbag, dropped them, and picked them up. Her battered car was parked against the opposite footpath, and as she ran across the road, she was nearly knocked down by a green and white Eastman's delivery van heading in the opposite direction. Livia dodged across a second lane of oncoming traffic, wrenched her car door open and jumped into the driver's seat. She jammed the key into the ignition and started the engine with a rattle and a roar.

It had just turned half-past seven. The radio news bulletins were still jammed with reports about the Minivers, but these no longer made sense to Livia, so she turned them off. She pulled out into the traffic on Queen Rosamund Boulevard and drove off without putting on her seatbelt. Eight blocks down, she had to stop at the traffic lights outside the palace. While she was waiting in the turning bay, the big iron gates slowly opened and a plain white car pulled out of the driveway.

"Oh, no, *no*!" Livia beeped her horn at the familiar profile behind the wheel, but Madame had turned into the heavy traffic on Miniver Boulevard and the peak-hour rush was carrying her away. Livia flicked on her indicator and wrenched her steering wheel hard to the left. There was a blare of horns as she forced her way out of the turning bay and drove through a red light. A car scraped her bumper as she crossed the intersection and Livia felt her face turn scarlet. She hoped the other car was not badly damaged. Luckily her own was so old that another scrape would make no difference.

The white car was moving swiftly through the traffic, changing lanes and getting further away from her. Livia drove as quickly as possible, but as the two cars left the centre of town it became harder and harder to keep up. The white car passed the university and the golf course, and crossed over a railway line. At the level crossing, Livia was stopped by the boom gate, and had to watch as her cousin drove up the hill and disappeared.

"Oh, rats." Livia sat gloomily, waiting for the long goods train to go past. By the time she got over the crossing, there was no way of telling which direction Madame had taken. Livia drove up the hill and down the other side. And at that moment she saw exactly where her cousin must have gone.

Months before, when Madame had first returned to

Artemisia, Livia had gone with her to a strange building. It was a kind of arch at the end of one of the city's bridges, with a door like a house and several rooms inside. Madame and Livia had been looking for a missing key. Apparently, it had belonged to Papa King, and since he had once used the bridge to store things in, Madame had hoped it might be there. She and Livia had searched but found nothing. Now, as she drove towards the river, Livia glimpsed the arch over the tops of some trees, and knew Madame must be there.

Sure enough, the white car was parked at the foot of the archway. Livia turned off the main road and drove down the bumpy driveway. When she reached the bottom she parked her car beside Madame's and got out. No one answered her knock. The door was unlocked, so she turned the handle and went inside.

"Cousin Karen?" Livia's voice floated up the dusty stairs. The place seemed even nastier than it had the last time she had visited. Livia put her hand on the rail and started to climb. Above her she could hear raised voices, but she could not recognise them or understand what they were saying. At the top of the stairs was a landing with a low door. Livia was about to knock when her cousin's voice spoke loudly on the other side.

"I'm getting tired of this, Millamant. I don't think you understand what a dangerous position you are in. After

133

all, nobody cares about you. The whole city thinks you killed the Minivers. If they found your body in the river tomorrow, there would be general rejoicing."

A small raspy voice replied, so softly that Livia could scarcely hear. Without thinking about what she was doing, she leaned forward and put her ear to the door.

"Is that a threat, Karen?" the raspy voice said. "Why don't you just finish me off, and have done with it?"

"Because I want to know where the key is!" Madame shouted. "You know that, you miserable *dwarf*! Why don't you just give me what I want?"

"I am *not* a dwarf." The other voice was weak, but dignified. "I've said I don't know where the key is. Even if I did, I would never tell you. I know what it means, you see. I know why it was kept from you. You and your mother tried to kill Papa King. He couldn't bear to have you locked up, so he sent you away. But I was there. I was working in the archives when it happened. I saw *everything*."

"Where is the key, Millamant?" said Madame. Her voice was matter-of-fact now, in a way that Livia found more chilling than her threats. "I need to know, and I have no more time to waste on you. I'm sure you understand."

"The key is wherever Rosamund put it," said

Millamant. "Believe what you like, but that is my final word on the subject."

"If I were you, I'd be careful about using the word 'final'," Madame began, when suddenly something awful happened. Livia, whose nose had been twitching from all the dust, gave an enormous and unexpected sneeze.

"Who's that?" said a third voice, and the door in front of Livia was thrown open. Before she had a chance even to squeak, a sandy-haired man grabbed her by the dustcoat collar and dragged her into the room.

"Who are you? What are you doing here?"

"I'm Livia Wallace," Livia stammered. "Madame's cousin. I – I've come to talk to her."

"Livia?" Madame pushed forward. "What is it? What are you doing here? Have you found the Most Secret Room?"

"No. Not yet – I mean, I'm not certain." Livia did not like the tone in her cousin's voice, any more than she liked being manhandled. "I went to the palace, but you were just leaving, so I followed you. I found this." She held out a tiny object, a dainty, heart-shaped diamond ring, embellished with a sweeping *R*.

Madame took the ring and turned it in her fingers. As she did, something happened inside Livia's head. Perhaps it was the conversation she had overheard, or maybe it was simply the expression on her cousin's face.

Madame had never been pretty, but Livia had drawn many portraits, and knew that sometimes even the plainest people could look beautiful. It all depended on what was going on inside their head at the time. The expression on Madame's face now was one of the ugliest Livia had ever seen. Livia was sure that, despite her size, Rosamund Miniver was neither weak nor helpless. But she suddenly knew, with immutable certainty, that until she understood exactly what Madame was doing, that she could not hand her over into her cousin's keeping.

"Where did you find this?"

Livia hesitated. She had, of course, found the ring on Rosamund's finger, but she could not say that without first explaining that she had caught and tied her up at the archives. Wishing that she was better at telling lies, she said, "In the archives, on one of the lower levels. I found a backpack, too, but I didn't bring it with me."

Madame's face lit up. "That's all I want to know," she said. "Ron, this is a definite sighting. Put a team together and go to the archives as quickly as possible. Does anybody else know about this?" She turned to Livia, who shook her head. "Excellent. I want you to drive back to the archives and wait for Ron. Show him where you found the bag and the ring, and do whatever else he asks you to. Do you understand?"

"Yes." Livia backed away, and ran down the stairs.

Fortunately, Madame did not appear to have noticed how upset she was. By the time Livia reached her car, she was crying.

The drive back to the archives was horrible. Several times, Livia nearly ran off the road, and all the time she was terrified Ron would get there first. When she arrived, she found nothing had changed. The archivists were about their work, the porters were wheeling trolleys full of files, and the first researchers were poring over documents in the Reading Room.

Livia ran straight down the stairs to the basements. On the fifth level she found Gibraltar. He was searching the storeroom where Rosamund had been hiding, frantically burrowing into the pile of boxes and throwing the empty ones over his shoulder. When he saw Livia he started.

"I'm sorry, do you need something—"

Livia shook her head. "It's Rosamund," she said. "They're coming for her. We have to get her away."

12

MINIVERS FAN CLUB HQ

The Minivers Fan Club was the largest Minivers club in Artemisia. It was not the only one, of course. There was the Friends of Rosamund Club, the Minivers Music Circle, and the Emily Forever Society. But the MFC was, and had always been, the most important. From its tiny beginnings in Lindsey Smith's living room it had grown to fill a purpose-built headquarters with two levels of offices and a warehouse at the back.

The MFC warehouse had a cement floor and a metal roof, and was jammed with cartons containing all sorts of Miniver merchandise. Fans could write in for Rosamund tea towels, Emily baseball caps, CDs and posters, books and fridge magnets. Finally, there were the toys. Whole bays of steel shelving were filled with Miniver dolls, jigsaws and board games of every description. Among the boxes in this section was one that had arrived from Eastman's department store just before the warehouse closed. It sat in the darkness like all of the others, but with one important difference. There was no packing tape on the outside. The box had been sealed from within.

Suddenly a huge kitchen knife came stabbing through the box's side. It jiggled about, sawing noisily through tape and cardboard, and there was the sound of heavy breathing as the small person wielding it worked hard to force their way free. A foot kicked through, the cardboard flew apart, and Emily Miniver's head poked out and looked around.

Emily sighed with relief. The warehouse was closed up and deserted. Travelling there in the box had been a tremendous risk. She had been afraid she would be dropped or suffocated, or found by the driver. There had also been a very real danger that her box might be opened when it arrived at the club. But now her gamble appeared to have paid off. After a hot, bumpy and very frightening journey, she had been wheeled inside the warehouse and simply left there.

Emily climbed out of the box. For about a minute she stamped and stretched to get rid of the cramps. Then she reached into the box, pulled out her backpack and switched on her torch. After the *Bella-Mae*, Emily was too nervous to turn on the main lights in case somebody saw her from outside, but she knew the general layout of the building, and had very particular things she wanted to investigate. Something strange and treacherous was obviously happening at the very highest levels of the club. But Emily had another, equally important reason for coming here. She might have failed to find Lindsey Smith, but she knew that among the thousands of members of the Minivers Fan Club there were plenty of people who would help her. If Emily could get into the main office, she would be able to find their addresses and phone numbers in the records.

Emily made a quick detour to the warehouse toilet and had a drink of water out of the tap. Then she went back into the warehouse and looked everything over. The door into the main office was locked, but there were also several windows at the top of the wall that divided the warehouse from the office. Emily was sure that, if she could reach them, she would be able to climb through into the upstairs offices. The problem was getting up there. Luckily, she had already thought of a solution.

At the end of the first aisle was an electric forklift that the warehouse volunteers used for ferrying heavy boxes. Emily put a carton on the platform behind the controls and climbed on to it. A battery of lights lit up across the control panel when she pressed the start button and she tentatively pushed the biggest handle upwards.

The forklift jerked forward. Emily was thrown off

balance. Immediately she let go of the controls and the forklift came to such an abrupt halt that she was nearly pitched on to the floor. For several minutes Emily drove the forklift haltingly around the warehouse. Controlling it was not as easy as it looked. It spun around at the lightest touch of the steering wheel and the fact that it was dark inside the building did not help. But after a little practice, her steering improved. Emily drove over to a pile of empty wooden pallets, and, after several tries, managed to pick one up. Then she drove the forklift to the office wall and carefully parked it beneath the window.

The next bit was the worst part. For a few minutes, Emily experimented with the forklift's arms, moving the empty pallet up and down until she felt confident she knew what she was doing. Finally, when she was ready, Emily pushed the LIFT control forward and jammed her torch against it to hold it in place. With an electric whine, the forklift's arms began to rise. Emily leaped down and ran as fast as she could to the front of the machine.

The pallet was already almost out of reach. Emily jumped up and grabbed hold of the edge. The motor strained as it caught her weight and the pallet shifted on the fork. For a moment, Emily swung dangerously back and forth. Her legs kicked furiously until she managed to get one up on to the pallet. All this time, the pallet was sweeping upwards. Emily closed her eyes and clung on with all her strength. Her left leg was dangling in empty space; she was half on, half off the pallet, but she dared not shift her position. If she fell now, she would be killed. With a shuddering jerk the arms reached their full extension and stopped. Emily opened her eyes. The pallet had come to rest just short of the open window.

Emily pulled the rest of her body on to the pallet. It swayed horribly, and there was an agonizing jab as a splinter went into her arm, but she could not stop until she had worked her way across the shaky wooden platform to the window. Emily reached up with one hand and grabbed the sill. She pulled herself into a kneeling position, shoved the sliding window fully open, and gingerly rose to her feet.

The room beyond was shadowy and deserted. Emily swung first one leg and then the other over the sill. Her feet dangled for a moment and she dropped triumphantly on to a leather sofa under the window.

"*Ooof!*" Emily hit the sofa like a trampoline and bounced on to the floor. She had done it! She had actually done it! As soon as she had recovered her breath, Emily felt her way to the light switch and stood on a chair to turn it on. At once, she knew where she was. The committee boardroom was furnished with a conference table and several bookcases full of books with titles like *The Minivers Fashion Book*, and *The Minivers: Their True Story*. But tonight there was something Emily had never seen in the room on her previous visits. A huge collection of Miniver dolls, the big, life-sized sort, had been taken out of their boxes and lay jumbled in a heap on the floor.

The dolls' glass eyes glinted up at Emily from beneath their eyelids, and while she stood in astonishment, wondering who on earth had done such a creepy thing and why, she heard voices in the downstairs foyer. Emily snapped off the light again. Several people were heading up the stairs from the lower office; there was no time to get away. Emily hurried over to the pile of dolls and burrowed in between several plastic bodies. She had just settled into place when the door opened, the light switched on, and the smell of freshly cooked pizzas floated into the room.

"Put the food on the table, Holly."

Emily quailed a little under the heap of dolls. She had instantly recognized Titus's voice, and indeed, there he was, not ten paces from her, dressed in his usual black jeans and Minivers T-shirt with the sticking plaster still on his forehead. He was accompanied by three people Emily did not recognize: a man in a suit, and two women, one dark-skinned and pretty in a tight red shirt,

143

the other with a face like a sheep. The pretty woman put several pizza boxes on the table and started to open some tins of beer and soft drink. At that moment two more people entered the room. Emily saw Ron, her old Chief of Security, and her heart sank even further.

"Go and eat your pizza, Fiona," said Titus.

Fiona, who was a girl about Emily's own age, scuttled into the room and opened a pizza box. She had limp brown hair and a plain face, and for some reason looked familiar. Fiona put a piece of pizza on a paper plate and curled up on the sofa not far from where Emily was hiding. The grown-ups sat down around the table and everyone started to eat.

For the next ten minutes there was hardly any conversation. The pizzas were ham and cheese, and supreme with pineapple, which were Emily's favourites, and the warm delicious smell was almost as much as her empty tummy could bear. At last the pizza boxes were pushed aside. Fiona produced a book and started reading.

Titus, who was obviously in charge, called everyone to attention and opened a folder. "On with our meeting, folks," he said. "I don't need to tell you we have a lot to get through tonight. Ron, in particular, has some exciting news for us, and Len here has come from the palace with some news about getting money out of the

Minivers' bank accounts. First things first, though. Holly, you're in charge of coordinating the reports. Would you give us a run-down on how the search is progressing?"

"Thanks, Titus. Can everyone take a set of these photocopies?" Holly stood up and handed the copies around. "If you'll look at these sheets, you'll see I've compiled the reports from the police, the Minivers Crisis Line, and Ron's security team. The pink page lists what we believe to be genuine Minivers sightings. It's pretty hard to mistake a Miniver for an ordinary person, so most of them should be reliable. The yellow sheets are lists of possible places the Minivers have been.

"Now, you'll see on the pink page that there have been no definite sightings of Rosamund since she escaped at the beginning of the week. That makes it very likely that she is being helped by someone—"

"I have some information on that," volunteered Ron. Everybody looked at him expectantly. Emily felt suddenly faint. "As a matter of fact, we've tracked Rosamund down to the City Archives. One of the porters seems to have been hiding her in a storeroom. By the time my people got there, they'd both disappeared, but we're on the porter's trail. His name is—"

"Gibraltar," said Titus.

"That's right." Ron stared at him in surprise. "That's his nickname. His real name is Peter Barnabas. They tell me he writes books."

"I don't think too many people read them," said Titus dryly. "Tell me, what are you doing to find him?"

"I've put a team on to it, of course," said Ron. "But I have to tell you again, Titus, this can't go on indefinitely. I've had the entire security force working around the clock. Every friend, every fan who might help the Minivers has been chased up; we've done face-to-face interrogations of over two hundred people. We've searched every possible hiding place you suggested, right down to their favourite dressmaker. It can't continue at this pace. We simply don't have the resources."

"It won't be for very much longer," said Titus. "Rosamund's whereabouts have always been the biggest mystery, and we're on her trail now. As for Emily, she was picked up last night on a security camera at Eastman's store in George Street. It's fairly obvious she's been hiding there during the day and only moving around after dark."

"What if Emily gets help, like Rosamund?" asked the second woman fearfully. "The fan club has twenty-five thousand members. You never know who could be helping her."

"I'm aware this is a problem, Brenda," said Titus. "As a matter of fact, Phase Two of our operation will be dealing with this issue directly; it should be launched very soon. If it's as successful as I hope, then we can expect support for the Miniver sisters to pretty nearly disappear. Meanwhile, Emily's very young, and she's not used to being on her own. I admit, she's been more resourceful than we expected. But she's obviously still in the city, and she has no way of leaving it. She can't take buses or trains, and she's lost her car. She needs food, clothes and shelter. But I think we're all forgetting the most important thing of all. The Minivers need each other."

From her hiding place, Emily saw Fiona's shoulders stiffen. She did not say anything, or even look at Emily directly, but Emily realized without doubt Fiona had seen her. Emily's muscles tensed. She waited to be seized and hauled into the open. But nothing happened. Meanwhile, Titus continued talking, his face intense with concentration.

"The Minivers love each other more than anybody else in the world. From the moment of Emily's arrival, they have never been apart. But there is another bond that makes their love for each other go even deeper. Without her sister, each Miniver is unique. Separated, she is also totally and terribly alone. By now, I think

Rosamund and Emily will be starting to understand this. For this reason, the one thing they will both be doing now is trying to find each other.

"And that, my friends, is how we are going to find them. Tomorrow, there will be an advertisement in the newspaper. Not a big one, but big enough to be noticed. It will tell Rosamund Miniver that if she wants to be reunited with her sister, she will come to a rendezvous at a place I have specified. If she doesn't, she will never see Emily again."

"What if Rosamund doesn't see the advertisement?" asked Ron. "She might not come. And what if Gibraltar comes with her?"

"If Gibraltar is with her, she will certainly see the ad. As for the other possibility, I'm sure you'll be able to plan for that."

"No," said Ron. "I'm afraid I won't. Before we go any further, Titus, let's get this straight. I'm not doing this for love, or because I'm too stupid to understand what's really happening." He looked contemptuously at Holly and Brenda. "I'm doing this for money. One hundred thousand Artemisian dollars. That's what I was promised, and so far I haven't seen a cent of it."

"You'll be paid," said Titus. "As soon as we have the Minivers."

"I'll be paid now," said Ron. "You need me, Titus.

Without me, you would never have been able to kidnap Rosamund. Without me, the whole thing finishes here. My son, Alex, needs an operation so that he can walk. There's no other way for his mother and me to find the money. I don't like what I'm doing, but if handing over two spoiled brats who never lifted a hand to help me will give my boy a chance, then I have to take it. But I'm not like you. I know the difference between right and wrong, and if I don't get what I want from you, I'm out."

"If that's what you really think of me," said Titus softly, "you should be a very worried man." There was an unpleasant pause, in which nobody said anything. At last Titus turned to the man in the suit, who so far, had not spoken. "Len. Do you have any money in that briefcase?"

Len nodded. "I have ten thousand dollars."

"Then give it to him," said Titus, "and all of you, come with me down to the main office. I want to show you the first things we've printed for Phase Two."

The moment the adults left the room, Fiona put down her book and got off the sofa.

"You'd better come out," she said. "I know you're in there."

Emily hesitated, then climbed out of the pile of dolls. Fiona was standing with her hands on her hips, dressed in shorts and a faded blue T-shirt from which Emily's own face stared out. The girl still looked oddly familiar, thought Emily, though she could not work out why. Meanwhile, Fiona regarded her with interest and, Emily realized to her surprise, some satisfaction.

"I always knew you were the clever one," Fiona said. "How ever did you get here?"

"I had myself delivered," said Emily. "In a box." As she said this, her words sounded unexpectedly funny. Her mouth twitched, she started to laugh, and then Fiona started giggling too and neither of them was able to stop.

"Oh, goodness," said Emily, clapping a hand over her mouth. "They'll hear!"

"Wait here," said Fiona, and went out of the room. Emily heard her trainered feet running down the stairs. A minute went by before she heard them running back again. By this time, Emily had managed to stop herself laughing. Fiona came into the room and locked the door behind her.

"It's all right," she said. "They're in the main office, looking at some posters and talking about Phase Two, whatever that is. It should be a while before they finish. What are you doing here, anyway?"

"I'm looking for information," said Emily. "I didn't realize anybody else would be in the building. What about you?"

Fiona's face fell. "I'm here with my mum," she said. "She's on the committee, but I don't think she really understands what she's got herself into. Brenda. She's the one who looks like a sheep."

"Oh."

"A *nice* sheep," said Fiona defensively. "She's very kind, really. Only I'm afraid, she's not very bright, and Titus can make her do whatever he wants. He even persuaded her to help kidnap your sister. He told her how much she would enjoy having Rosamund in her house, and she believed him."

Emily blinked. "Rosamund was in your house?"

Fiona nodded. "She was there after the kidnapping. Holly and Ron were the ones who did that; my mum just drove the van. Rosamund stayed with us for a little while and then she escaped. I helped her. Are you all right?" she asked, as Emily turned white and sat down suddenly. "You look like you're going to faint."

"Sorry," said Emily in a wobbly voice. "It's just this is all such a shock, and right now I'm so terribly hungry I can't even think straight. I've eaten nothing but nuts and biscuits for three days."

"You poor thing!" Fiona was appalled. "Look, here's

some leftover pizza. I don't think it's gone cold yet. I'll get you a soft drink, too." She shoved a slice of ham and cheese pizza into Emily's hands and started rattling through the drinks tins to find a full one. Emily bit ravenously into the pizza. After a diet of sugared almonds and shortbread biscuits, it was indescribably delicious.

There was a soft pop as Fiona opened a tin of lemonade. "Goodness!" she said, as she turned around. "You *are* hungry!"

Emily popped the last bit of pizza into her mouth and reached for the lemonade. "Never mind about me. Tell me about Rosamund. You said you helped her. How?"

"Well, Mum left us together, and Rosamund asked me to leave her alone for a moment," Fiona explained. "I knew she'd escape. There was a big hole in the flyscreen. She climbed out while I was in the kitchen."

Emily sighed. "Thank you so much," she said. "You can't know what it means to me to know she's safe. You see Rosamund – she's not very brave. And she gets worked up so easily and does silly things. The night it happened, she was already very upset."

"I know." Fiona's face went pink. "I was there, at the party, when it happened. I was the one who upset her."

Emily put down her drink. The birthday party at the

Artemisia Hotel now seemed so long ago that for several moments she found it impossible to remember any details. Then a half-remembered impression swam into focus: a girl with an autograph book, excitedly shaking Rosamund's hand. "So that's where I recognize you from!" Emily exclaimed. "Of course! Titus said your mother was on the MFC committee. No wonder you looked familiar."

"I didn't mean to hurt Rosamund's feelings," said Fiona, in a voice of great distress. "I wasn't even thinking what I was saying. It was awful. When she burst into tears, it was like I'd stuck a knife into one of the people I love best in the world. And then my mother helped kidnap her, and everything was worse than ever. I felt I owed it to her to help her. And I'll help you, too, if you'll let me."

"You don't have to help me," said Emily. "Just don't give me away. If I can get out of here, I'll manage the rest somehow. If I can find Rosamund before she gets to the rendezvous, I can warn her—"

"You'll never do it," said Fiona. "Not on your own. Look, it's Friday now and the fan club is closed for the weekend. You can hide here overnight. I'll come back tomorrow with the ad and we can work out what to do." She stopped. "What's the matter? Don't you trust me?"

"It's not that," said Emily, and she burst into tears. All

her life, she had believed that Minivers were for people to love. Papa King had always said so and Emily had taken him at his word. But for the first time, Emily was beginning to realize it was not that simple. All week, the love she had taken for granted had been slipping away to the point where she was beginning to doubt it was hers at all. When Ron had mentioned his son Alex, Emily had wanted to curl up and die of shame. Three years ago, Alex had been hit by a car and left in a wheelchair. Emily knew she and Rosamund could have paid for any number of operations for Alex, yet it had never once crossed their minds to do so. How many other people had she treated like this, and still expected them to love her? Emily did not know, but in her heart she was honest enough to recognize that she had failed at what she most believed in. She had let down, not just her fans, but herself.

"Why are you crying?" asked Fiona anxiously. "Was it something I said?"

"No," said Emily. "I just don't understand why you want to help me when I don't deserve it."

"Deserve it?" said Fiona. "What's that got to do with it? Wanting to help doesn't come out of people's heads. It comes out of their hearts, because they love you."

Emily shook her head. "I used to think that. I don't know any more if it's true."

"It *is* true," said Fiona. "Don't you understand? All my life, for as long as I can remember, I've wanted to be like you. I know I'm not pretty, or clever, or talented. My dad ran off before I was born, and Mum's never had a proper job or any money. But when things were bad you were there, showing me it could get better. When they found you in the basket, you were small and unimportant and had nothing. But you proved that someone like that could become important. That the smallest girl, whom nobody wanted, could do amazing things. That's why your true fans love you, Emily. We love you, not for what you do, but for who you are. We love you because deep down, in our hearts, you give us hope."

Emily looked up at her. Despite her shabby appearance, there was something solid and trustworthy in Fiona's face that reminded her of Millamant. It was like a light glowing deep within her. At the sight of it, the fear that had been growing in Emily's heart, and that had almost beaten her, suddenly shrivelled and died.

"Thank you," she said simply. "Thank you." And she reached up and took Fiona's hand.

13

THE KEY

Rosamund sat on the sofa, dressed in one of Livia's T-shirts, drinking a cup of milk. It was raining heavily, the sort of drenching storm that usually heralded the start of summer in Artemisia. Rosamund felt very thankful to be inside. There was something homely and comforting about Livia's house, and she had slept last night in Livia's grandparents' big old bed, feeling safer than she had since her kidnapping.

But feeling safe was not the same as feeling peaceful. All week, Rosamund had been living on her nerves, and she knew her problems were not over. At first, she had hoped that someone would stop what was happening, and that she would be able to go home and resume her normal life. Rosamund was now starting to understand that this was unlikely to happen. The old days at Miniver House were gone, possibly for good, and what lay ahead was difficult, unpredictable and dangerous. At best, it was a life full of all sorts of inconvenience. Rosamund was starting to discover how unpleasant it was to have to stretch to open doors, to have to climb on to chairs to get things off tables, to have to fetch heavy and bulky items for herself. But the worst thing of all was the prospect of being alone, with no Emily to share her troubles. Rosamund missed Emily desperately. She had shed many frightened tears on her behalf and, in her worst moments, was convinced she would never see her or Millamant again.

The front gate creaked open, and a car rattled down the driveway and parked. Rosamund heard its door slam and the sound of footsteps running up the steps on to the verandah. Gibraltar came out of the kitchen and opened the front door for Livia. She shook out her umbrella and came into the house, carrying several shopping bags and a basket, from which protruded a slightly damp newspaper and a loaf of bread.

"Nice weather for ducks," she said, putting down her shopping. "I've got the bread and some fresh fruit, so we can have lunch shortly. And I've bought you some clothes, too," she added, handing Rosamund one of the bags. "They're probably not what you want, but they're the best I could do."

"Thanks," said Rosamund. "It will be nice to have something that fits." She took the bag into the bedroom and shut the door. Meanwhile, Gibraltar picked the paper out of Livia's basket and sat down on the sofa.

"Hmm," he said. "I see our small friend's disappearance is finally off the front page. I wonder if they're running out of things to say?" He folded his feet up under him and began reading an article. Livia kicked off her wet shoes and sat in an armchair. She was feeling very down, and though she tried to tell herself it was the weather, she knew in her heart it was not.

"Oh, no!" wailed a voice from the bedroom. "This is *so* embarrassing."

The bedroom door opened and Rosamund emerged. She was wearing a short yellow dress with roses embroidered around the hem. In her hand was a pair of pink and white check shorts, and a white T-shirt with a flower on it.

"Look at me!" said Rosamund tragically. "I look *awful*. And these pink shorts are even *worse*."

"It's not that bad," said Gibraltar. "I think you look rather cute."

"Yes – if I was two years old." Rosamund looked at her feet, which were encased in a pair of white sandals, and shuddered. The sandals had been made for a baby's fat little feet. Even with the lacy-topped socks which Livia had thought to buy with them, they were far too broad.

"They don't even fit properly!"

"Well, I think you're very ungrateful," said Livia

crossly. "I did the best I could. Everything for very little girls is like this. You're lucky I didn't buy you ducks and bunny rabbits." Her eyes welled up, and she angrily dashed away a tear. Gibraltar shot Rosamund a stern look.

"I'm sorry, Livia," said Rosamund. "I didn't mean it to sound that way. But you have to understand, I'm not used to this. Normally, my clothes are designed especially for me. Having to wear things like this is . . . a bit of a come down."

"I'm afraid you'll have to get used to it," said Livia. "Oh, dear. What are we going to do with you? The longer you stay here, the more dangerous it gets. Gibraltar, do you think we could possibly smuggle Rosamund out of Artemisia altogether?"

"Smuggle me out of Artemisia?" Rosamund was horrified. "You can't do that. Emmie and Millamant are still here. I can't possibly leave without them." She turned to Gibraltar. "You won't make me leave, will you? Millamant is a prisoner, and we don't know even know where Emily is. I'm not leaving Artemisia without her, I'm *not*."

"Calm down," said Gibraltar. "Nobody's going to make you leave Artemisia. Speaking of Emily, though, can you shed any light on this for me?" He folded the paper in half twice, and held it out.

Rosamund followed his pointing finger. On the left-hand side of the page was a small boxed advertisement.

> IF THE PERSON the Key
> was given to at the Artemisia Hotel
> on Saturday 9th returns it to its
> rightful owner, it will be to her
> sister's advantage. K16, tonight,
> Monk and Wharf Streets. 8.30 p.m.

"Last Saturday was my birthday. They're talking about my party." Rosamund's eyes widened. "They've got Emily!"

"They want you to think that, anyway," said Gibraltar. "Personally, I think it's a trap."

As he spoke, Livia took the paper from him and read the advertisement with a furrowed brow. "What's this key they're talking about?" she asked.

"Oh, I don't know," said Rosamund impatiently. "Just some stupid old thing Papa King sent me for my birthday. He's gone a bit funny in the head, poor darling. I don't think he knew what he was doing. It was cut right down the middle; it wouldn't even have worked."

"Cut down the middle?" said Livia. She put down the paper, looking suddenly anxious and pale. "Rosamund, you don't have the key with you, by any chance?"

"No," said Rosamund. "It was left behind at Miniver House, when I was kidnapped. I gave it to Emily to put away."

"But it was definitely cut in half? Right down the middle, lengthways?"

"I think so," said Rosamund. "Why? Is it important?"

"There is a room in the City Archives, where the most secret documents are kept," said Livia. "Things Papa King doesn't want anyone to know. The key to that room was made in two pieces that must be put together to open the door. One piece is held by the City Archivist. The other belongs to Papa King, or whoever else is king or queen of Artemisia.

"Since Papa King fell ill, nobody knows where the Most Secret Room is. Cousin Karen has had me hunting for it secretly. She told me it was because there were records there that showed how badly Papa King treated her, but I don't believe that any more. I think she wants to get in there for another reason. And I know she has been searching herself for Papa King's key."

"What for?" asked Rosamund, puzzled. "And why on earth did Papa King give it to me?"

"Whoever holds the key has a very strong claim to be Papa King's successor. Cousin Karen knows that. I think she wants the key so she can become queen herself. I also think," said Livia, "that when Papa King sent you his half of the key, he was doing more than giving you a birthday present. I think he was saying that he wants you to be the next queen of Artemisia."

"Oh, *no*." Rosamund stared at her in horror. "You mean, this is why all this is happening? What on earth was Papa King thinking of? He can't be serious, I'm only fourteen."

"Papa King was seventeen when he succeeded his mother, old Queen Rosamund," said Gibraltar. "You are his eldest foster daughter, named in her honour. You are also one of the two most popular people in Artemisia. It's not so outlandish an idea as you might think."

"But I don't want to be queen," insisted Rosamund. "I'm not interested in ruling Artemisia. I would be absolutely hopeless. Papa King must have had another reason for giving me the key. As far as I'm concerned, Madame's welcome to it. I'm going to go to that rendezvous and tell her so."

"No!" exclaimed Livia and Gibraltar together. "You mustn't – you absolutely mustn't!"

"But she says she's got Emily!"

"It's a bluff, Rosamund," said Gibraltar. "She's trying to trap you. Even if she had Emily, do you really think she'd hand her over?"

"She won't hand her over if we don't go," said Rosamund stubbornly. "We have to try. It's up to you whether you come or not, but if I ignore this ad, and that awful woman does something to Emmie, I will *never* forgive myself."

"That's quite enough, Rosamund," said Gibraltar. "If you're determined to go, then of course, we will go with you. We're certainly not going to let you go alone. But you must promise that if we do, you will do exactly what I tell you. Is that agreed?"

"Oh, all right," said Rosamund. She picked up the paper again. "K16. I wonder what that means? Do you think they're talking about a map?"

"*Sssh!*" said Livia suddenly. "There's somebody coming up the path!" She stepped out briefly on to the verandah, then shot back inside with a face as white as paper.

"It's Cousin Karen," she whispered. "They've found us!"

Madame walked down the path in her tight new shoes, feeling rather uncomfortable. It was a long time since she had been to her grandparents' old house, and she was astonished to see that her cousin Livia had painted the outside walls bright yellow. She also seemed to have planted a lot of unnecessary flowers in the garden. Madame walked up the front steps, opened the lattice gate on to the verandah, and rang the big brass bell. A moment later, the door opened.

"Hello, Cousin Karen. What's the matter?"

"I need to talk to you," Madame explained. "May I come in?"

She followed Livia into the living room and stopped dead in shock. Inside, the house was even more amazing than the outside. Madame stared at paintings of flowers, a jumble of china ornaments, the vivid pink sofa. The ceiling was painted blue with fluffy white clouds. The whole effect made her feel rather nauseous. "It's very . . . bright."

"Yes," said Livia. She picked a newspaper up off the sofa and quickly tossed it underneath. "I like it like this. Please, sit down."

Madame sat down opposite Livia. She had not been looking forward to this visit, and if Livia's help had not been vital to her plans she would certainly not have been making it. Madame hated visiting people. Her idea of a good time was to sit at home by herself in the dark, eating out-of-date gingernuts and watching reruns of black-and-white movies. Madame especially liked old science-fiction films, the sort where the monsters had rubber tentacles and invaded Earth in cardboard spaceships. She enjoyed the way the monsters would hide in swamps and then jump squelchily on people's faces, and she approved of the fact that the film companies had not wasted any money on special effects. Sometimes, in the most exciting part of a movie her cat would come in with a mouse she had caught and crunch it up on the threadbare carpet. Madame would stroke the creature's fur and tell Kitty, in between ray-gun shots, that she was a good girl for saving money on cat food. All this was great fun, and much easier than visiting a relative she secretly found rather peculiar.

Livia cleared her throat. She knew the polite thing to do was to offer Madame a cup of tea, but since she did not want her visitor to stay any longer than she had to, she did not suggest it. Instead, she said, "How can I help you, Cousin Karen?"

"Livia," said Madame solemnly, "I got the impression yesterday that you were a little bit upset. I was afraid that you might have overheard something that was said, and, er, well believed it."

"I – I didn't overhear anything," stammered Livia. "Honestly, I don't know what you're talking about."

Madame looked at her suspiciously. She was so dishonest herself that she normally did not find other people's lies surprising, but Livia had always been so helpful and trustworthy that it struck her as odd that she should start fibbing now. Madame was certain Livia had been on the landing outside the tower room when she had threatened Millamant, and that she had overheard Millamant's remark about the plot to kill Papa King. It was the only way of explaining why she had been so upset. Madame knew that it was vital for her to keep Livia on side until the Most Secret Room was found. If she did not and Papa King died, the City Archivist would go to the Most Secret Room to look for

Papa King's will. All the secret records of that long-ago plot would come to light, and Madame would be exposed as a would-be murderer.

Livia shifted uncomfortably. "Is there anything else, Cousin Karen?"

Madame forced a smile. "As a matter of fact there is," she said. "I wanted to tell you how grateful I was that you came to see me yesterday. Your help means a great deal to me and – well, Livia, I was thinking we should get together more often. There's a really good movie on TV tonight. It's called *The Claws of Arachnea*. I was wondering if you would like to come to the palace and watch it with me."

"Oh," said Livia. "Thank you. That would be – lovely."

"Come at half-past six. I'll give you dinner," said Madame recklessly. As she stood to leave, her eyes fell on a small T-shirt and shorts that were draped on the arm of the sofa. She picked them up and looked at them curiously. "What's this for?"

Livia froze with her hand on the door knob. "Just a present. A friend of mine's had a baby."

"They look a bit big for a baby," said Madame, frowning.

"Yes. They were, er – cheap."

Cheap was something Madame could understand. She smiled at Livia and put down the clothes.

"Tonight at half-past six, Livia," she said. "I'll look forward to seeing you then."

14

THE HOUSE OF MIRRORS

Saturday afternoons were busy at the Artemisia Funfair. Though badly run-down, it had been a popular place for families since the days of old Queen Rosamund. On sunny weekends the funfair was filled with children eating ice-creams, and riding on merry-go-rounds and dodgems. The air rang with screams and laughter, and towering over everything the Big Wheel turned constantly, its carriages soaring up and swooping down again to the accompaniment of a hundred different tunes.

But by late afternoon, most of the families had gone home. The evening visitors tended to be rough boys, who hung around in gangs and spent their money on shooting galleries and the fastest rides. None of them were interested in a mousy girl who arrived at the Wharf Street gate with a heavy wheeled shopping bag, shortly before six o'clock. The girl stopped and bought a pair of plastic glasses and a huge rainbow-coloured wig from a hawker on the pavement. When she had put on her disguise, she wheeled her bag through the gate and disappeared into the crowds.

Fiona was feeling scared. Last night, when she had promised to help Emily Miniver, she had felt brave and rather important, but she had not had time to think about what she was doing. It was only later, at home, that Fiona realized what she was actually up against. The Minivers' enemies were determined to catch them. The funfair would be filled with Ron's trained security team, and Fiona would have no way of telling where they were. Most of all, though, Fiona was afraid of Titus. Normally he paid her practically no attention, but that would quickly change if she got in the way of his plans.

A small "ouch" sounded inside the wheeled bag as it went over a rock. Fiona's heart bumped in fright, but she kept her face as expressionless as possible behind her silly glasses. She reached the end of the first avenue of attractions, and turned into the next one, pausing occasionally to admire the stalls. At the Minivers House of Mirrors, Fiona stopped and took careful note of the stall number that was painted in tiny characters above the empty ticket booth. Then she walked casually over to a nearby foodstall, bought two Dagwood dogs and two tins of soft drink, and wheeled her bag to a low wall at the furthest edge of the fair.

Fiona unzipped the top of the trolley. With a watchful eye on the passers-by, she slipped in a tin of lemonade and a greasy bag containing one of the Dagwood dogs.

The paper bag rustled and there was a muffled pop as the tin was opened. A small voice spoke cautiously from within. "Did you see anybody?"

"I didn't recognize anyone," whispered Fiona. "But of course, I don't know any of the people from your security team, except Ron. I did find K16, though. It's the Minivers House of Mirrors."

"The Minivers House of Mirrors?"

"Yes. It's full of those trick mirrors that make thin people look fat, and fat people look thin. It was closed up, so I couldn't get in. I didn't want to hang around, in case somebody noticed me."

"Good thinking." Emily pulled the Dagwood dog out of its paper bag, sniffed it once, and shoved it back uneaten. She sipped restlessly on her lemonade. Nervous excitement bubbled away inside her, making it hard for her to keep still. Close as she was to a breakthrough, there would be more danger for her in the next few hours than at any other point of her adventures. The hardest part was not knowing what Rosamund was doing.

Emily closed her eyes and tried to think like her

sister. Rosamund was impetuous and wilful, but she was not stupid. In a tight situation she would try to charm and wheedle her way out, but when that didn't work, she would swiftly change tactics and try to bargain. The problem was that without Papa King's key, Rosamund had nothing to bargain with. Emily reached into her T-shirt, where the half key dangled on a string around her neck. She did not know why it was so important, but she hoped she could use it to buy their freedom. The trick would be to do this without being caught or double-crossed first. There were so many things that could go wrong. If Rosamund failed to notice the advertisement; if Ron or Titus recognized Fiona under her silly wig; if somebody saw her moving about inside the bag, then all would be lost. There was not much hope. But without her sister, Emily knew she could not go on. Without Rosamund, she would rather be dead.

The interior of the bag was growing dimmer. Pinpricks of red and gold light started shining through the weave in the canvas, and Emily realized that the funfair coloured lights were switching on. Suddenly, the shopping bag wobbled. Emily heard Fiona stand up, and her voice whispered, hoarse and excited, through the unzipped flap.

"Emily! I think I've just seen Rosamund, in a stroller. She's here!"

At half-past six precisely, having left Rosamund and Gibraltar to make their way to the railway station, Livia arrived at the Artemisia Palace for her dinner with Madame.

Livia had never been to the palace for dinner before. Aunt Susan, Madame's mother, had thought herself too grand for the rest of the family, and Livia and her parents had never been invited. As an usher led Livia down the marble corridors, she tried hard not to stare. The furniture had the sort of expensive look she had only seen in posh magazines, and there were portraits and sculptures everywhere.

The usher led Livia up a sweeping wooden staircase and stopped at a door. She knocked, and announced, in a formal voice, "Miss Livia Wallace."

"Come in, Livia dear." Madame was at the window, looking out at the city lights. The door snapped shut behind Livia's back, leaving her alone with her cousin. "Welcome to my little home."

Livia opened her mouth and quickly closed it again. She had intended to say hello, but the air she breathed in had brought with it such an overwhelming stink of old vinyl shoes and used cat litter that she almost choked. Livia wanted to run away. She knew she was a bad liar, and she did not want to spend a moment more in her cousin's company than was absolutely necessary. But she, Gibraltar and Rosamund had agreed she must go along with Madame as if nothing had happened. "She mustn't guess that you've been helping us," Gibraltar had said. "Keep an ear to the ground and be as friendly as possible. You might learn something we don't know."

"G . . . good evening, Cousin Karen," Livia managed. "Thank you so much for inviting me." She looked anxiously around the room, which was a strange mixture of new and pretty curtains and wallpaper, crumbling furniture, and hideous knick-knacks. A tortoiseshell cat came slinking past her leg and Livia forced herself to smile and pat its head. The cat hissed and clawed at her. Livia thought it looked as if it had worms.

"Don't mind poor Kitty," said Madame. "She's very shy – like me, aren't you darling?" She picked up the scrawny animal, making chirping noises that made Livia feel like throwing up. "Sit down, dear. Our yummy dinner's on the table: it wouldn't do to let it go cold."

She gestured Livia to the table and whipped the cover off a huge silver tureen with the air of somebody offering her guest a rare treat.

It was tinned tomato soup.

"We're running late," fumed Rosamund, as she and Gibraltar hurried up the hill to Central Station. "It's half-past six: we'll miss the train!"

"You were the one who held us up," Gibraltar protested. "I still don't know why you had to cut your hair off."

"Because it made me look too much like a Miniver, of course," said Rosamund. Her magnificent hair had been cropped, close to her head, and she was dressed in a pale blue romper suit and hat. "Oh, please, hurry! We're never to going to make it!"

"I'm going as fast as I can," panted Gibraltar. "It's all right for you. You don't have to push this pram."

"*I'm* not heavy," said Rosamund. "You just have to run faster. Anyway, it's your fault for not letting Livia drop us off in her car. I'm sure it would have been safe, and we'd be there now!"

As she spoke, Gibraltar crested the hill and started running down the other side. He too, was looking rather strange this evening, for he had lost his beard and completely shaved his head. In the gathering darkness he and Rosamund might just pass for a father with his baby boy. If they could only get there in time. . .

The station clock chimed the half hour. Cars beeped and slowed as Gibraltar ran across the road and entered the station concourse. A long-distance express had just

173

come in and there were people everywhere, flooding through the gates in the opposite direction to the one they were going. Gibraltar ploughed through the crush, running over toes and scattering angry passengers.

"Platform Six!" shouted Rosamund, glimpsing a departure board. Gibraltar raced through the last of the crowd and leaped on to an escalator with the pram balanced precariously on its two back wheels. There was a sound of electric motors starting up below them. Rosamund leaned anxiously forward, and saw a silver train waiting at the platform at the bottom.

"It's there! We're going to miss it!"

"Hold on!" yelled Gibraltar. He flew off the escalator on to the platform and ran for the nearest carriage. The doors snapped shut in their faces. The guard blew his whistle, the train rolled away, and Rosamund and Gibraltar were left behind.

The tomato soup had been taken away, and a dish of rice pudding had been set down on the table. It was gluggy, and smelled of slightly sour milk. Livia stared at the bowl in front of her and wondered how on earth she was going to eat it.

"Did you enjoy your dinner, Livia?"

"Er – yes, thank you, Cousin Karen," said Livia, finally realizing that the extremely nasty soup had actually been dinner, and that there was to be no main course. She lifted a spoonful of pudding to her mouth and nibbled it. "I'm sorry . . . I think I'm feeling a little bit full."

"I've made some changes in the kitchens since I came here," said Madame in a satisfied voice. "It was quite appalling, the waste that went on there. Luckily I've found a wonderfully thrifty woman to replace Papa King's chef. She can make a meal out of almost anything."

"Really?" Livia squished the rice pudding about with her spoon.

Madame nodded and reached for a second helping. There was a curious excitement about her tonight, and she kept looking at the clock. "Livia," she said solemnly, "something very important is going to happen tonight. Something that's probably going to change the history of Artemisia. The fact is, we have found the key to the Most Secret Room."

"The key?" Livia did her best to look surprised, though inwardly she had begun to shake. "What wonderful news. You must be very pleased, Cousin Karen."

"Well, as a matter of fact, I don't have it yet," Madame

admitted. "But I'm assured it has been found, and the important thing is that it's going to be brought to me tonight. I thought you might like to be here when it arrives."

"But we don't know where the Most Secret Room is yet," said Livia. She could think of nothing but Rosamund and Gibraltar, heading into what was now obviously a trap. "Why do you want the key? What are you going to do with it—"

"That's none of your business, Livia," said Madame sharply. "All that matters is that the key will be in my keeping. Goodness me, look at the time. *The Claws of Arachnea* is about to start. Sit down on the sofa, there's a good girl, and take your pudding with you. It would never do to waste it." She turned on the ancient TV, and a ghostly black-and-white picture slowly came into focus.

In a distant part of the palace, a clock chimed seven. . . .

Inside the bag, bumped, jolted, and thrown around, Emily was starting to feel sick. She had no way of telling what was happening. Once or twice she had peeked out and glimpsed a tall man pushing a stroller through the crowds, but it was hard to see more when she had stay out of sight. Then Fiona started to run. Emily lost her balance and fell over, and in the process she completely lost track of where they were and who they were following.

The tin of lemonade had spilled and was sloshing about in a sticky puddle on the vinyl base. The Dagwood dog smelled greasy and revolting. At last Fiona came to a halt and tipped the shopping bag into an upright position. She flipped back the lid and Emily rose shakily to her feet.

"Have you lost them?"

"Not exactly." Fiona pointed to what looked like a moveable building. "They went in *there*." Emily looked at the shabby door and realized it was the rear entrance to the Minivers House of Mirrors.

"Help me." Emily reached up her arms, and Fiona lifted her out of the shopping trolley. Her legs were so wobbly after being crouched inside that for the first few seconds she could barely stand. But the moment had come. If she was to find Rosamund, Emily knew she had to face whatever was on the other side of that door.

"I have to go after them," she said. "Alone. You keep watch here. If anyone comes, try and let me know, but don't do anything dangerous. At the first sign of trouble, go straight home."

"You're not going in there alone!" protested Fiona. "Titus and Ron will be waiting. They'll catch you!"

"And if you come with me, they'll catch you, too," said Emily. "I'm small, and I'm used to hiding now. They might overlook me: they won't miss both of us. You *must* do as I ask, Fiona. Promise me, as my friend, that you won't try and follow."

"All right," said Fiona. "I promise. But I still don't like it. And if they do catch you, I'm not going to let them get away with it. I'll do something, never mind what. I've got a few ideas of my own."

"Let's hope we won't have to use them," said Emily in a shaky voice.

Fiona dropped to her knees and they hugged one another. There was a brilliant flash of light and a loud explosion overhead. Emily started, and looked up.

"It's the firework display," explained Fiona. "It must be seven o'clock. They always have one here at that time on a Saturday."

"Good," said Emily. "It will be a distraction." She let Fiona go, climbed the steps to the door, and slipped inside.

As Fiona had guessed, the Minivers House of Mirrors was a sort of maze filled with black curtains and trick mirrors. The moment the door closed behind her, Emily slid behind the nearest curtain and waited to see if there was anyone around. Luckily, her arrival seemed to have gone unnoticed. When her eyes had grown accustomed to the poor light, she pulled the curtain aside and peeped out. The Minivers House of Mirrors was closed for the night, but somebody had left lights burning: dim, red lamps, that cast a creepy glow over the expanses of wavy glass and black material. Emily shivered. A false step now could end everything.

Emily stepped out from behind the curtain. She felt as if eyes were watching her from behind every drape, and she had barely gone half a dozen steps when something moved in the darkness in front of her. Emily almost screamed, but realized just in time she had simply glimpsed her own reflection in one of the mirrors. It would have made a normal-sized person look like a Miniver, but Emily was so small that her reflection was no bigger than a cat's.

Step by step, ducking behind curtains at the slightest sound, Emily made her way into the maze's heart. The space was not big, but it was designed to be confusing, with curtains doubling back in dead ends, and giant cardboard cut-outs of chairs and other furniture hanging from the ceiling, Emily guessed, to give ordinary people some idea of what it was like to be Miniver-sized. The mirrors reflected back hideous images of herself: first fat, then thin, then stretched to almost normal size. But the creepiest things of all were the waxworks. At almost every turn stood life-sized models of Rosamund and herself, dressed in copies of their own clothes and posed on wooden pedestals. The wax faces were doll-like, with grinning mouths and exaggerated make-up. The eyes, which were made of glass, seemed to glitter as Emily passed.

And then, as she tiptoed around yet another length of curtain, she saw something in the shadows up ahead. Emily's heart began to pound. A baby's stroller, exactly like the one she and Fiona had followed, stood parked in a swathe of curtain. The canopy was down, but there was a small person sitting in the seat, and a single lock of long black hair flowed over its shoulder and down the stroller's back.

"Rosamund?" Emily risked a whisper. There was no reply. At once she knew something was wrong. In four quick steps Emily reached the stroller and jerked back the canopy. A wax model of Rosamund smiled stupidly up at her. And then a voice Emily knew spoke close behind her.

"Hello, Emily. Nice to see you."

Livia sat in agony on the sofa. The rice pudding congealed like concrete in her stomach and further down, the tomato soup was gurgling through her intestine. Worst of all, *The Claws of Arachnea* was one of the most terrible movies she had ever seen. Its main character was a woman with black lipstick and a bathing cap covered with plastic spider webs. Her henchman wore eyeliner and a raincoat. They lived in a palace made of silver-painted cereal boxes and were holding the world to ransom with radioactive rubber spiders. Livia knew she had to get away.

She cleared her throat. "Cousin Karen," she whispered through the darkness. "Do – do you think I could use your toilet?"

"Shhh," hissed Madame. "You're spoiling the best bit!" She grabbed Livia's arm. Arachnea's henchman released the spiders on an unsuspecting world.

Livia thought of Rosamund and Gibraltar, and tears of helplessness and terror rolled down her cheeks.

"Titus," said Emily.

Titus smiled. "Hello, Emily. I knew you'd be here, sooner or later."

He stepped out from behind the curtains. In the red glow of the downlight, the cut on his forehead showed as a puckered scab, the sort that would leave a permanent scar. Emily took a step closer to the stroller containing the fake Rosamund and clutched its frame. For the first time she saw that she was at the very end of the maze. Beyond Titus, a swing door made of thin black rubber led out into the real world. It might as well have been made of solid steel.

Titus followed her gaze. "The door's guarded," he said. "Just in case you're thinking of running off. But I don't think you'd try that, Emily. You're clever enough to understand how thoroughly I work now. Besides, Rosamund is probably on her way here. There's no way you'll leave while there's a chance of finding her."

"Why are you doing this?" whispered Emily.

Titus rubbed his hand along the frame of one of the nearby mirrors. His reflection showed in it, distorted, looming. "You might find this hard to believe, but I'm doing it because it's fun."

"Fun?"

He nodded. "Yes. It's like a game, you see. The best game in the world. You tell people lies and they believe them. You trick them and trap them into doing things, and they don't have a clue how it happened. Think of Brenda, for instance. You've no idea how much fun it was persuading her to kidnap your sister. Then, there's you. I tricked you into thinking I was a Minivers fan. I'm sorry, Emily. I'm afraid I've always thought you and

182

Rosamund were rather boring little people. You can't sing very well, or dance particularly gracefully. In fact, I'll tell you a secret. If you weren't the size you are, nobody would ever give either of you a second glance."

"For somebody that boring, you've gone to a lot of trouble to catch me," said Emily. Her mouth was dry, and she was clutching the stroller so hard her hand hurt.

Titus shook his head. "Not at all. That's what's been so much fun. If Holly and I had caught you and Rosamund that night at the railway station, we would have handed you straight over to Madame and that would have been the end of it. But you surprised us. You ran away, and all of a sudden everything got really interesting. Have you and Rosamund ever played hide-and-seek, Emily? Isn't it the best feeling, when you're trying to work out which cupboard the other person's hidden in? You have to put yourself inside that person's head, and think of where you would hide if you were them. Sometimes you pretend to go away, and they'll even come out of hiding. That's what this is all about, you know. A game. But tonight, I win. You thought tonight's trap was for Rosamund, but all along it was really for you."

Emily's heart skipped a beat. "For me? Why me?"

"Because you have Papa King's key," said Titus. "I need it. I know you have it. Give it to me now, and I will let both you and Rosamund go."

"You might have tricked me once; I'm not silly enough to let it happen again," said Emily. "Anyway, the key was given to Rosamund, not me. I don't even have it."

"Oh, come on, Emily," said Titus, and for the first time, Emily thought he sounded annoyed. "Don't mess me about. We've searched Miniver House from top to bottom and the key wasn't there. It wasn't on Rosamund when she was kidnapped, and Millamant claims to have no idea where it is. That means there is only one person who can have it. You."

"I don't have it," repeated Emily. "But I'll make a deal with you – on my terms, not yours. Let me and Rosamund leave Artemisia completely. As soon as we're safely over the border, I'll tell you where the key is hidden."

"Nice try, Emily," said Titus. He started walking towards her. Emily retreated behind the stroller. "But there's something you're forgetting. You're a Miniver. You're small. You're weak, you're fragile, and I happen to know you're lying. Hand the key over now. If you don't, I'm going to make you, and we both know that won't be pleasant—"

"You can't make me do *anything*!" Emily screamed at the top of her lungs and with all her strength she shoved the stroller forward. It hit Titus square in the shins and with a furious cry he tangled and tripped, bringing it down on top of him. Emily dropped her head and ran. The swing door opened ahead of her; she saw coloured lights and heard snatches of music. Two men rushed towards her, but they were coming into darkness and she was already upon them. Emily shot between their legs like a bull through a matador's cape.

"*Fiona! Help! Help me!*"

The rubber spiders were breeding in a deserted graveyard. Arachnea and her henchman were going to take over the world. Madame was sitting on the edge of her seat, when the telephone rang. "What a nuisance!" she exclaimed. "Excuse me, Livvy, please."

Madame got up and went into the next room. The phone stopped ringing and Livia heard her talking angrily to someone called Ron. It was now, or never. Livia jumped to her feet, grabbed her handbag, and ran.

Fiona was nowhere to be seen. Emily had left her at the back of the building and come out at the front where there was no help, only straggling crowds of funfair visitors. A narrow gap led between the Minivers House of Mirrors and the adjacent chair-o-plane to the alley at the back. Emily ran down it, yelling Fiona's name, but before she had gone more than a few paces another guard leaped over the chair-o-plane's fence. It was Primrose, in a purple shirt and jeans. She had a peculiar-looking gun in her hand and she lifted it and took aim.

Emily heard something buzz past her left ear and ping off a metal hoarding. Instinctively, she dropped flat. She rolled under the chair-o-plane's chain fence, and fled beneath the flying feet of the people on the ride. Joined by the two men from the Minivers House of Mirrors, Primrose leaped back over the fence in pursuit. As the three of them scattered around the ride, Primrose fired her gun a second time. A woman bystander gave a strangled cry and collapsed in a heap, with what looked like a dart in her arm.

Emily ducked under another set of railings. She plunged beneath the canvas sides of a knock-down stall and blundered into a basket of coloured balls. A woman screamed and a man tried to grab her shirt. Emily evaded their clutching fingers, and somehow squirmed under more canvas into the next booth. She ran from one stall to the next, tripping over struts and tables and dodging grasping hands. Then she reached the end of the row of attractions, and there was nowhere else to go.

"She's here!" shouted a voice. Emily ran for the nearest clump of people. They were lining up for the Big Wheel, and as she burrowed into the crowd, hoping to hide from her pursuers, the ride stopped and the queue began to move. Emily was carried along with it, up some steps and on to a metal platform. As Emily emerged from the crush at the end of the line, an empty car swept down to the platform.

"There she is! Stop her!" Titus and the guards were running up the exit stairs on the other side. Emily dodged between the attendants' legs and jumped into the empty car. The safety gate slammed automatically shut behind her and she swung away gracefully into the air.

There was shouting on the platform below her. Emily looked down. Ignoring the shouts of the attendants and the screams of the other passengers, Titus jumped on to the struts of the wheel and began climbing determinedly in Emily's direction.

Step by step, strut by strut, Titus's black-clad figure moved towards her. Emily could hear people screaming, though whether because of her, or Titus, it was hard to know. The wheel turned slowly to nine o'clock, then ten, then eleven. Titus was about two cars below her. Emily ran from one side of the car to the other, like a fly trapped in a bottle. The car rocked dangerously on its pivot. A hand appeared on the footplate, followed by another. Emily screamed. A pale blond head bobbed up, and with a last, powerful heave Titus was standing on the footplate and struggling with the gate.

The latch was on the inside. Emily punched at his hands with her little fists, but there was no stopping him. The door swung open and Titus was in the car. The cut on his forehead had opened up again. It was bleeding, and his face was savage.

Emily shrank back against the safety bars in the opposite corner. The car had reached the top and was starting to go down again, but there was still a long way to travel. Titus took a step towards her. He was staring at her throat, where Papa King's key had worked its way out of her shirt and was dangling on its string. Emily glanced hopelessly at the ground. A crowd had gathered at the foot of the wheel and people were shouting, pointing upward. They looked tiny, but as the wheel swung down they grew larger and larger, until suddenly a bald man swam into focus. He was pushing a pram and scattering the crowd in front of him. Emily heard a shrill, familiar scream and saw Rosamund stand up in the pram, her great dark eyes staring upwards in horror.

"*Emily!* Jump! Jump! Gibraltar will catch you!"

Titus lunged. There was a sharp snap as the string holding the key gave way, and Emily saw the key in his fingers. A moment was all she had. She jerked up the catch. The gate opened and Emily swung out with it into space and fell.

Lights whirled and streaked in the darkness; there was a rush of air and speed. It was nothing like flying, only sheer and utter terror. Emily closed her eyes and tensed and then, like a cricket ball into the hands of an expert keeper, she landed with a heavy smack in someone's arms.

"The street!" yelled Rosamund. "Gibraltar, you've got to get out of here! Head for the street!"

Emily opened her mouth to draw breath and was thrust, roughly and unceremoniously into the pram beside her sister. The man who had caught her wrenched the pram around and sprinted for the Wharf Street gate. It bounced and jolted over the uneven ground, and Emily and Rosamund grabbed hold of each other and clung on for dear life.

People were staring, some were cheering. The stone posts of the gate were not far ahead. Gibraltar put on a burst of speed. Primrose jumped out from behind the gatepost. She was lifting her peculiar gun when a girl appeared from behind a hawker's stand, cannoned into Primrose's legs and brought her down.

"Minivers for ever!" shouted Fiona. "Go Emily!"

Gibraltar ran through the gate on to the footpath. A

small yellow car was driving along the street. As its driver saw them, it swerved to the kerb and the passenger door was flung open.

Rosamund scrambled out of the pram. She shoved Emily into the back of the car and Gibraltar bundled her in from behind. A dart from Primrose's gun ricocheted off the rear panel, then he leaped into the front seat and slammed the door.

"Go, Livvy!" shouted Rosamund. "*Step on it!*"

Livia put her foot on the accelerator. With a screech of rubber, and a belch of exhaust fumes, the car accelerated up the hill and sped away.

15

MINIVERS ON THE RUN

"So you see," said Titus, "in the end, there was really nothing more we could do. They had outside help we weren't expecting. Somebody in a car. It was white or yellow, we didn't get the number plate. We think the driver must have been Gibraltar's friend."

Madame sat at the desk in her palace office, her plain face made ugly by jealousy and disappointment. The evening, which had begun so perfectly, had gone completely to ruin. She had not even been able to see the end of *The Claws of Arachnea*. Titus stood on the other side of the desk in his usual down-at-heel trainers and black jeans. His expression was cool as a cucumber, and there was something about it Madame did not like. She reflected that there had always been quite a lot she did not like about Titus, though she could not have put her finger on exactly what it was.

"They got away, then."

"Yes."

"Both of them."

"Yes."

"And the key?" said Madame, her voice rising in fury. "You told me I'd have the key by this evening. What about it?"

Titus spread his hands apologetically. "I'm sorry."

"You should be more than sorry," said Madame. "You came to me a year ago promising a great deal, and I've had nothing so far in return. I'm too angry to speak to you now. Get out."

Madame waited until Titus left the room, then pushed back her chair. It was late and the palace was in darkness, but there was one more person she wanted to speak to. Madame locked her office and walked to a distant suite of rooms. There, in a darkened bedroom, an old man lay propped up on pillows in a hospital bed. Tubes and wires snaked away under the bedclothes, connecting him to a machine that whirred and clicked. There was a flicker of light across a monitor and the soft hiss of an oxygen bottle.

The old man's hair was silver with dark streaks still in it. He had a high forehead and a beak of a nose. His eyes were closed, but at the sound of Madame's footsteps, they opened, and gradually focused. Madame came and stood at the head of the bed.

"You thought you were being very clever, didn't you,

Papa King?" she said. "Giving that key to Rosamund Miniver. Did you really believe I wouldn't know what it was? Did you honestly think I'd let you get away with giving a Miniver something that should have been mine?

"Well, I'm going to tell you something. You're never going to see the Miniver sisters again. I've left them exactly where you left me: without friends, without money, without a future. And when I get the key back, it won't matter what you've written, or what you've said, or who's helping you. You're finished. You and your precious Minivers are over."

Papa King lay in his bed. He said nothing, for he could not speak, but his dark, old eyes looked up at Madame as if she was something small and contemptible. Under his gaze, Madame felt as a weak person always feels when they stand before a strong one. Fear and anger gripped her. Her hand fumbled furiously for the switches on the machine beside his bed – and then she saw the twitch of Papa King's lips, and realized he was laughing at her.

Madame's hand clenched and dropped to her side. She leaned forward and hissed in his ear.

"One of these days, Papa King," she said. "One of these days – I'm going to *pull your plug!*"

Titus walked down the palace steps with his hands in his pockets. The half-key on its bit of broken string sat snugly in the palm of his right hand. As he crossed the deserted car park he could see, in the distance, the long dark shadow of the abandoned Miniver House. He turned out of the palace gates into Miniver Boulevard and headed for the river.

Dream your dreams, Madame, Titus thought. *Become Queen of Artemisia if that is what you want. I will put you on Papa King's throne: I don't want it for myself. And when you are there, I will trick you and lie to you, and through you I will fool and lie to the whole of Artemisia. You and I were made for each other. All in all, I think we're going to have a lot of fun.*

At the end of the street, Titus stopped to look out across the river. A night wind blew over the water, ruffling his bleach-blond hair. A memory came back to him, of Emily Miniver shaking her fist at him from a boat. The game of hide-and-seek was not over yet.

He smiled, and walked off alone into the night.

On the outskirts of the city, a small yellow car turned off the main road and sped towards the mountains. The car climbed into the foothills, its engine straining. The road grew darker and narrower and the trees closed overhead and became a forest.

"You can come out, now," said Livia, from the driver's seat. "There's no one following us. I think we should be safe."

Huddled together on the floor behind Gibraltar's seat, Emily and Rosamund threw off the blanket they were hiding under. There was not much room on the back seat, even for Minivers, but Emily did not mind the squeeze. With Rosamund beside her, her heart was full of happiness. It was Rosamund, truly Rosamund, and the smell, the feel and the sight of her were so right and familiar that Emily could do nothing but cry.

"Don't cry, Emmie," said Rosamund, hugging her. "It's all right now. It's all right."

"Oh, Rose," said Emily. She ran her fingers over her sister's newly shorn head. "Your poor hair."

"Never mind," said Rosamund. "It'll grow. Anyway, I was due for a change of image." She blinked back her own tears. "I can't believe you're here. I thought I'd never see you again. I thought you were dead."

"I thought you must be, too," said Emily. "I – I couldn't bear it."

"Never again," said Rosamund fiercely. "Nothing, *nothing* must ever separate us again."

"No," said Emily, with a strength that welled up from

somewhere inside her and made it a promise. "Nothing ever will."

She thought back over the terrible trials through which they had passed. In little more than a week, she and Rosamund had lost their home, their possessions, their friends. They had learned about betrayal, had suffered fear and want and despair. Nothing, though, had been as bad as the thought they might lose each other. In her heart, Emily knew the old days were gone for ever. They could never go back, but they could still go on together.

"It won't be easy," she said aloud, "but we'll do it somehow."

"We Minivers may be small," said Rosamund, "but we're tough."

More miniature mayhem in. . .

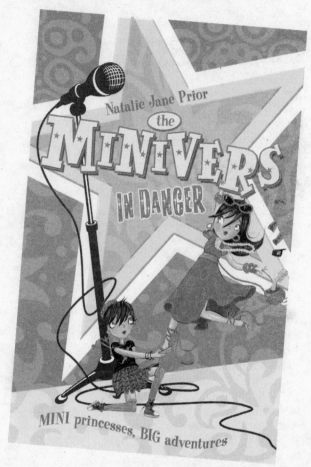

Natalie Jane Prior

the

MINIVERS

IN DANGER

MINI princesses, BIG adventures

. . .coming soon!